Pride Publishing books by Elizabeth Hollows

Single Books
Return to Duty

I0570500

RETURN TO DUTY

ELIZABETH HOLLOWS

Return to Duty
ISBN # 978-1-83943-905-6
©Copyright Elizabeth Hollow 2020
Cover Art by Louisa Maggio ©Copyright July 2020
Interior text design by Claire Siemaszkiewicz
Pride Publishing

Published in 2020 by Pride Publishing, United Kingdom.

RETURN TO DUTY

Dedication

To the friends and family who are always excited to hear about my latest story. You've waited a while for this one, but I hope you like it.

Chapter One

Jaybird was an outlaw. His mugshot showed a wink and a smirk, and he was never seen without his beat-up old hat. Jay found his way out of trouble with charm and flirtation. He was a nuisance, not a thug. He lounged lazily at bars and chatted up any pretty person who walked by. Jay stole treasures as often as he stole hearts, and while he'd traveled through much of the galaxy, it was the moons of Asam that he enjoyed the most.

Asam's moons were known for many things. They were the last place in the universe where a person could get a good martini, the best place in the galaxy to end up in a brawl and the one place in the quadrant that ignored universal laws. A rich Qui named Hezon Taziv owned the moons. He applied his own rules and it allowed the rocks to be neutral territory. It was the perfect place for Jay to relax after a successful heist.

He'd been spending his time on the moon Vicente these last few weeks. It had a nice diner that employed a handsome waiter who Jay was attempting to get to know better. The waiter's name was Bryce, and he was as confusing as he was attractive. He'd flirted with Jay for almost three weeks, leaning against the counter, bantering playfully. Bryce would push them just shy of a kiss but Jay had been waiting for him to give in. Yet, a week ago, he'd stopped all conversation. It had taken a day for Bryce to go from nearly falling into Jay's lap to ignoring his existence. It made little sense. Jay rarely met someone who puzzled him. People were typically cut-and-dried, with obvious motivations and desires. Bryce wasn't so simple, and Jay wanted to work the man out. No one had intrigued him like that for a long time.

Jay normally hopped between planets, indulging in attractive bodies while letting his latest arrest warrant lose its heat. He never stuck around. He never formed attachments. Adventure, lust and curiosity were his main motivators. People weren't meant to factor into his decisions, yet Bryce had stolen his attention. He'd never said no, and he'd never told Jay to back off. He'd just changed without a word.

Jay couldn't leave Vicente without discovering the reason why.

If they were somewhere else, he might have believed Bryce had learned he was a thief and had been repulsed — but Bryce lived and worked on Vicente. Asam's moons were overflowing with opportunistic criminals. Bryce would have known what he was the first time Jay had walked into the diner. He'd never hidden it. Jay took pride in his roguish appearance. A lot of people wanted to bed a 'bad boy', and Jay was happy to fulfil their desires.

He'd thought Bryce was the same, given the way he'd flirted. Bryce seemed to want someone to shake him out of the working-class haze, maybe to get him a little dirty. The waiter was always pristine, with no hairs out of place. His uniform was a form-fitting sky blue that matched his eyes, and he wore a white apron that was always belted around his waist. Bryce had soft, almost feminine features that were highlighted by short, wavy black hair falling to just below his ears. He looked deceptively delicate, but Jay suspected that was a lie. Bryce wanted someone to take him on a wild ride that would leave him gasping.

He'd offered to take Bryce home the first night and give him exactly what he craved. Bryce had grinned and looked interested but had declined with a shake of his head. Jay hadn't been discouraged. The challenge of the chase kept Jay coming back.

The second night, Bryce had given back as many innuendos as Jay had offered and flirted with a competitive glint in his eyes. Jay had even invited Bryce back to his ship. The waiter had apologetically said no.

The pattern had never changed as the weeks had passed.

At first, Bryce had been too delectable to leave unravished, but soon, Jay looked forward to each evening. Bryce's personality was full of fire and his body was obviously gorgeous underneath that uniform. Jay had been certain it was only a matter of time until he would pin the waiter to the sheets.

But then everything had changed and Jay was still trying to get his bearings.

He'd been in the diner every night for the last week, but Bryce continued to ignore him. He'd stayed three hours on this occasion, and it was almost time for the restaurant to close. If Bryce was expecting him to leave along with everyone else, he was mistaken. There was nowhere Jay had to be. He could stay at the diner until morning.

Sprawled in a booth with his back to the wall, Jay's ankles were crossed and he rested them on top of the table's edge. There were a dozen other diners tonight — weary workmen from Asam, a few small-time thieves, the usual. Most of the waiters were chatting and leaning against the bar, but not Bryce. He moved around the diner with purpose and awareness — dropping nothing, cleaning counters and never forgetting an order. He cut an impressive figure as he weaved between the tables. Bryce's gaze flicked around the room, shining with an intelligence rarely seen in backwater diners. It was one more curious part of him.

Why does he work here when he could do so much better?

Jay watched it all from beneath the brim of his hat. He'd clasped his hands loosely and they rested over the buckle of his belt. He was pretending to be asleep and most of the employees believed it, but the sharp looks Bryce had been shooting him for the past hour showed exasperation. Jay had nearly smiled twice and given himself away.

The diner was slow to clear, but Jay was patient. When it was empty, Bryce would come over to rouse him and he would have the waiter's full attention. He might be able to get an answer out of the guy.

Jay was devising the best way to entice Bryce into a conversation. *A compliment? A flirtation? An upfront question to ask what the hell had changed his mind?*

A hard whack to his feet jolted Jay from his thoughts and caused his legs to tumble off the table and hit the cushioning of the booth. Jay jerked into a seated position. He pushed his hat back up on his head so he could look at the person who'd hit him. Bryce held a serving tray in his hand and looked unimpressed. The waiter had snuck up on him.

How did he do that?

Jay tried to recover his composure and charm.

"It's rude to wake the sleeping," he said.

"It's rude to sleep in a diner," Bryce answered. "And you weren't sleeping."

"Are you sure you know me well enough to tell the difference?" he asked, layering his words with flirtation.

The man didn't rise to the bait. Instead, he tapped his fingers against the tray.

"The diner is closed." Bryce made a gesture toward the door. "Please vacate the premises."

"'Vacate the premises'? I don't think I've been so politely thrown out of an establishment in years."

Yet, rather than do as requested, Jay relaxed back against the booth. Bryce narrowed his eyes.

"You should continue getting ready to close," Jay said. "I'm sure I won't bother anyone if I stay a little longer."

Jay anticipated an argument and already had a comeback prepared, but Bryce heaved a frustrated breath before turning on his heel. He started clearing dishes from the other tables and Jay watched on with surprise.

Will he ever act the way I expect him to?

More amused than suspicious, Jay settled in to watch the tight fit of Bryce's pants. There was something about Bryce that Jay couldn't put his finger on, but he wasn't worried. If his finely tuned survival instincts weren't concerned about Bryce, then he had nothing to fear. Jay had a gun, a nearby ship and a history of being in far worse scrapes than being ambushed by a waiter in a diner. It wouldn't even be the first time he'd turned a confrontation into a vigorous sexual marathon. Jay glanced at the counter. He'd had a few fantasies about a quickie in the diner.

Maybe I'll get lucky tonight?

The other waiters and waitresses shot Jay odd looks but they left him alone. Jay made a show of making himself more comfortable. It took ten minutes for the diner staff to leave but Jay barely noticed. He was far more interested in Bryce. The waiter busied himself with tasks until only his car remained in the lot. When he flipped off the lights, it left the diner with nothing but the energy lanterns outside for illumination. It gave the place an eerie, greenish-yellow hue and made the white of Bryce's apron glow. It was crumpled in one of Bryce's hands while a set of keys for a hovercraft was in the other.

Bryce stopped in front of him. Jay raised his eyebrows and let his gaze roam over Bryce's powerful thighs and thin waist. He was gorgeous. Jay wanted to strip him of every layer and explore what lay beneath.

"Will you leave now?" Bryce asked, annoyance in his voice.

Jay missed his former easy humor and flirtation.

"I could be convinced," Jay replied, "if I was leaving with you."

Bryce's cheek twitched — yet despite the weeks spent flirting with him, Jay still couldn't tell if it was a quelled smile or a pained grimace.

"I'm *not* leaving with you," Bryce stated.

"I'm good at changing people's intentions," Jay answered, undeterred. He added a smile full of promise and persuasion. "I can promise it would be worth your while."

Bryce rolled his eyes, but Jay glimpsed a spark of amusement.

"I have somewhere to be and someone to meet," Bryce said. He pointed at the door. "You need to leave."

Jay didn't move. He watched Bryce closely. "If you have somewhere to be, why are you still here with me?"

"The diner must be empty of *all* customers before employees can leave," Bryce said, stressing the 'all'.

Jay started to reply but stopped when he heard the unmistakable sound of a hovercraft approaching. Jay twisted and looked over his shoulder, widening his eyes. The craft was sleek and silver. It was an expensive ship that glinted in the light, making Jay's light-fingered hands twitch. Jay didn't know what it was doing on this side of the moon but he would be happy to relocate it. When the craft landed and the door opened, all thoughts of thievery fled from Jay's mind. There were only a handful of Quis on the moons of Asam and most of them were related to Hezon Taziv. Quis were notorious for their red hair, sharp teeth and dark skin. Jay wasn't stupid enough to frequent the moons of Asam without learning the faces of influential people who he should never rob. The youngest son of Hezon Taziv was one of those people.

What the hell is he doing on a working-class moon?

Bryce's sigh made Jay glance back at him. He looked frustrated — worried, even — and his gaze darted to the clock in the diner. It wasn't hard for Jay to put everything together and realize what was happening.

"He's the one you're meeting."

It explained a lot about Bryce's sudden change of behavior. Jay was many things, but he was not rich and

13

powerful like Zanik Taziv. Jay was impressed by Bryce's ambition, even if he was disappointed.

Bryce's attention flicked back to Jay. "I did mention having plans that didn't involve you."

Jay glanced at the Qui, weighing his options and how attractive the man was before suggesting, "Maybe a third person could make your plans even more enjoyable?"

Bryce shot him a cold and unimpressed glare, but the sound of a second hovercraft stopped Bryce from retorting. When Jay looked back this time, it was a black vehicle that approached. The Qui's body language was wary and uncomfortable. Whoever the new arrivals were, they weren't the rich man's friends.

Instinctively, Jay slid out of the booth, keeping wary eyes on the parking lot. His instincts were screaming warnings at him.

"Did you invite anyone else to your meeting?" he asked.

"No," Bryce answered, not looking away from what was happening.

The second vehicle hadn't quite landed when the passenger door opened and someone leaned out. They pointed an energy gun at the Qui and fired. The Qui collapsed and Jay placed a hand on Bryce's arm to keep him from moving or panicking.

"It was a stunner," Jay said. "He's still alive."

Jay didn't glance at the waiter. He kept his eyes on the unfolding scene. The craft had landed and the person who had shot the Qui exited. He walked over to the fallen man and stared down at him. The shooter held his weapon with an ease that spoke of familiarity. He was dressed all in black and had a mask over his face to further hide his identity. His only distinguishing feature was a ponytail of silver hair. Two other people joined him. They picked up the Qui effortlessly and carried him to the hovercraft. The shooter scanned the parking lot before his inspection caught on Bryce's hovercraft. He looked at the diner and Jay tensed. The man tapped his temple and something shimmered and shifted over his eyes. Jay recognized it and swore. *Command goggles.* They were the kind issued by the military and frequently stolen by criminals — and they had thermal sensing.

The man shouted an order to the driver of the vehicle, but Jay was already grabbing Bryce and yanking him backward in a mad dash and scramble over the diner's counter. Behind it was a wall with a servery that Bryce and Jay leaped through with a tumble and roll. They were both up in an instant. Jay located the garbage chute and started running. Bryce had the same idea, and they ran with desperation. They threw themselves inside — Bryce first, Jay second.

They tumbled down the chute before landing in the large steel bin below. It was made of tough metal, and Jay yanked down the lid. There wasn't a moment to spare as an explosion rocked the container and sent it hurtling away from the building and the inferno that had engulfed the diner. The pressure wave from the blast meant that they were slammed against the sides of the bin as it shifted and swerved. Their limbs collided with the walls as bags of garbage were tossed over and around them, splitting and covering them with filth. When the container finally came to a stop, Jay shoved the garbage away from his face and spat out something unpleasant.

Standing, Jay carefully lifted the lid, relieved that it hadn't buckled. He poked his head over the rim. They were a good few meters from the blazing diner, but Jay could still feel the heat from the fire. He was also far too close to people who wanted him dead. They needed to disappear.

Pushing himself out of the dumpster, Jay dropped onto the ground, keeping the bin between himself and the diner. He turned, planning to assist Bryce, but found that the waiter had already clambered out. Bryce kept a hand on the bin for balance as he stared at the inferno. Bryce would be shocked at what had happened and that they'd survived it—but they didn't have time to linger. Grabbing the waiter's upper arm, Jay tugged him away from the burning wreckage, hoping to get them as far from the area as possible. Bryce resisted him, but Jay just kept pulling.

"We need to get out of here before they see that we survived," he said. "We have to move, Bryce. My ship's not far."

Bryce hesitated for a few seconds before he turned into Jay's hold. They broke into a run as they scrambled across the rock and dirt that made up Vicente's terrain. The moon itself was barren, but it had fertile soil and a breathable atmosphere. That made it a tough place to call home, but it was useful for stopovers and industrial work. There was also a shuttle that ran from Vicente to Asam, which was popular with tradesmen and bachelors—people who wanted to get away for a few days and visit one, if not all the moons.

Jay hoped the popularity of traveling to and from Vicente would assist them. They didn't want to be noticed as they escaped. While his ship had cloaking technology, Jay preferred not to fly through monitored airspace with it, since the software had been obtained illegally. When they reached Jay's ship, he was grateful to find it was free from damage and hadn't been noticed by the kidnappers. Jay opened the doors and got them inside.

His craft wasn't large or luxurious. It had two sleeping quarters, a kitchenette and the piloting station. It was ideal for one person. Bryce would just have to make do while they were stuck together. He'd get the second sleeping quarters — if Jay couldn't convince Bryce to climb into bed with him. It would take a few weeks for them to reach somewhere safe if they wanted to get away from their attackers.

But that was a worry for when they were out of Vicente's airspace.

Closing the doors behind them, Jay moved to the piloting station with its well-worn seat and he started the ship.

"Won't they see us take off if we leave now?" Bryce asked, startling Jay. His hands were on the back of Jay's chair and he was eyeing the control panel suspiciously.

"No," Jay answered, shrugging off the unsettling feeling of having someone else on board. "I've altered the engineering for better stealth."

It had been a pain to do, but it had been worth it for the many times his cloaking devices and silent take-offs had saved his life and his freedom.

Tension still rested thick on Jay's shoulders as he maneuvered the ship into the air. Warnings about the explosion were flashing on the display, but Jay dismissed them and focused on looking for additional air traffic. He breathed a sigh of relief to see that the shooter's hovercraft was heading in a different direction. The attacking kidnappers likely believed that they were dead. The shooters would know otherwise once the news reports broadcasted a lack of bodies, but

Jay planned to be far away from Vicente by the time that happened.

"They're getting away," Bryce said, pointing at the disappearing hovercraft.

"That they are," Jay replied, while flying the ship in the opposite direction. "We should do the same."

"They have Zanik."

Jay grimaced. Wherever the Qui was going, it wouldn't be a pleasant experience for him, but the use of a stunner offered some hope.

"They'll have taken him for blackmail or ransom," Jay explained. "They kept him alive, and that bodes well for his eventual rescue."

"You're just going to leave him with them?" Bryce demanded.

Jay shifted with discomfort but tried to ignore it. He concentrated on the map of the area, needing to find a suitable place to uncloak the ship where no one would notice. He could feel Bryce's glare burning a hole in the side of his head the longer he remained silent. Jay sighed.

"Look," he said. "I understand you're worried about him, but you need to start worrying about yourself."

"We escaped an explosion. He was kidnapped."

"And you're handling that spectacularly well for" — *a civilian*, his brain categorized, but he shook the word away—"someone who isn't used to this kind of lifestyle, but you don't go up against people like that. You don't even report something like that. They think we're dead, so we keep it that way."

Bryce made an aggravated sound and pushed away from Jay's chair, beginning to pace. Jay let him and did his best to ignore the waiter. Thankfully, Bryce seemed inclined to keep his mouth shut and process what had just happened, as well as Jay's comments. Jay knew that leaving the man to his thoughts wasn't the safest thing to do, but Jay didn't have the time to devote to him. He could deal with Bryce going into shock when they were out of the moon's orbit and able to put the ship into a star-jump.

Jay still expected more protests from Bryce as he uncloaked the ship and slipped into the outgoing traffic, but the waiter remained silent. His shuffling steps over the metal only stopped once they'd passed the border scan. Jay waited until they were in the safety of open space to turn the ship to autopilot. When he finally swiveled his chair so they could talk, he found Bryce right in front of him, his arms crossed and a glare on his face.

"Where are you taking us?" Bryce demanded.

Jay blinked. *No shock, no hysterical laughter and no panic attack from the explosion? Will this man ever cease to surprise me?*

"The next star quadrant," he answered. "It should be far enough away that no one will search you out." Jay mentally shuffled through his contacts. "I have a friend. He can set you up with some new documentation and some cash."

"What are you talking about? I need to get back to Vicente."

Damn, Jay thought, feeling a stab of pity. *He's in denial.*

Jay took a subtle, preparatory breath and kept his voice calm. "Bryce, you can't go back there."

The waiter's glare intensified and frustration was visible in every one of his coiled muscles and twitching fingers.

"Bryce," he continued, "those people will find you and kill you. You need to be far away when they learn you're alive. I'm sorry, but there's nothing to do but leave that part of your life behind."

"I need to be on Vicente," Bryce insisted. "Don't take me anywhere else."

Sensing the impending panic attack he'd expected earlier, Jay stood. He hoped that stepping away from the controls of the ship would allow Bryce to calm down and listen to reason. The waiter didn't need to know that the ship was on autopilot and could perform the star-jump without his help. They would be leaving Vicente, whether Bryce agreed now or not.

"I know this is hard to take in," he said, using a soothing baritone to try to keep the man calm, "but you saw what those guys did and what they're capable of. The best thing you can do is disappear. It will keep you and anyone you care about on Vicente safe."

"What about Zanik? I can't just leave him there."

"He'll be rescued," Jay said. "There are people trained to get hostages like him back."

And their attempts sometimes work, Jay added, bitter irony infusing the words. Zanik might get free, but Jay wasn't holding his breath. He wouldn't state the harsh truth to Bryce. That would only make things worse.

"Everything will be fine for him," Jay continued, "so focus on yourself."

It had been Jay's mantra for years — *focus on yourself*. Now Bryce would have to adopt it too.

Unfortunately, the waiter still seemed skittish, angry and unreasonable, but before Jay could try another tactic, his ship started to light up and beep at him. Jay spun on his heel and looked at his screen. His eyes widened in shock at what he was reading. He stepped up to the console, re-reading the information but still feeling disbelief.

Bryce came to stand beside him, but Jay didn't even know how to comprehend this himself, let alone explain it to a waiter who was miles out of his depth. He was being hailed by the Intelligence Agency.

The IA was a powerful branch of the Universal Collective. The UC had members from every nation and planet. They were the soldiers, politicians and activists who worked outside a single government or world in order to protect the universe. The Intelligence branch was the keeper of secrets, and the men and women who worked there held the keys to peace or war. Jay was stunned.

Why are they here?

He didn't know how to respond to their communication, but it didn't seem to matter, because before he could devise a reply, his ship shook. The agency's craft had grappled them and was pulling them onto the larger ship. They were being forcefully boarded, which meant the IA must know what had happened and assumed that it involved Jay and Bryce.

I'm screwed, Jay thought.

Looking over at Bryce, he could only stare at the waiter, unable to think of anything comforting to say. It had all been Bryce's fault, yet Jay couldn't blame him for their situation or Jay's impending life of imprisonment. Jay's libido had drawn him into sticky situations before, but this was the first time he'd gotten himself tied up in an explosion, a kidnapping and a government capture, all without even kissing the person he'd been chasing.

Briefly, Jay considered reaching for the waiter and pulling him into a quick, passionate last-hurrah of a kiss before IA threw him into a cell. But, once again, Jay was unimpressed to discover that of all the things he'd lost over the years, his conscience hadn't been one of them.

Chapter Two

Okay, Jay thought as the IA craft pulled his ship closer, *damage control.*

His past might be mottled by crimes and illegalities, but Jay hadn't been involved in the Qui's kidnapping. He could prove that. And even if his outstanding warrants weren't enough for the IA to let him go, they should at least hand him over to a local authority. His crimes were small compared to what the IA normally went after. They wouldn't be interested in him, and that meant he had a chance to escape later.

But he didn't want Bryce to get thrown into a cell with him because of bad timing.

"Look," Jay said, turning to the waiter. Bryce was reading the warnings but glanced at him. "We're being boarded by the Intelligence Agency, and that means they've worked out that we witnessed something on Vicente. So, when they question you, tell them you've done nothing and that you don't know me."

"I *didn't* do anything," Bryce said, sounding unimpressed.

"Good," Jay said. "But be less defensive next time."

He glanced at the warnings, which told him that they had only a few minutes before IA agents would force open the ship. It wasn't a lot of time to prepare Bryce for an IA interrogation, but it was all he had.

"You need to make them believe you," Jay continued, looking back. "Admit you were only interested in the Qui for sex or his money. It will go a long way toward clearing your name."

"Excuse me?" Bryce demanded, sounding, of all things, offended.

Maybe he doesn't like his plans being so transparent? Well, that's too bad.

"It wasn't hard to notice what you were after," Jay explained. "They'll recognize it too. They train agents to read people and discover their secrets. If you're honest from the start, they won't have a reason to suspect you." Jay did feel a glimmer of sympathy, but sometimes a person just had to grin and bear it. "I know you'll want to lie about using the Qui for his money, but—"

"I *wasn't* using Zanik for his money," Bryce snapped.

"Status, power, whatever you were after," Jay said dismissively, focusing back on his ship. "You need to bare your secrets to IA. You think they're dark and dirty? Well, the agency won't care. It will mean nothing to them. Just let them help you and you'll be better for it."

The silence stretched. The air was tense.

"And what about you?" Bryce asked.

Jay glanced at the waiter. He was watching Jay with unreadable eyes.

"You're telling me how to act, but what are *you* going to do?"

There was no point lying, and even if he was going down, Jay could do it with a smirk. "Oh, I'm sure I can charm my way out of some of my arrest warrants."

Bryce narrowed his eyes, but before he could reply, the ship jerked and shuddered. They were inside the IA's docking bay and the controls of Jay's craft had been swiftly overridden. A minute later, a team of four IA agents burst into the ship. The agents were in black and wore the infamous IA masks. The masks were standard military issue with top-of-the-range technology, but while soldiers in combat had bulkier items that could withstand the rough and tumble of battle, IA masks were thin and smooth. They were designed for stealth and to hide one's identity. The only agent with any distinguishing markings was the captain of the unit. He had two thin white lines painted on the right cheek of his mask to designate his rank.

Jay put his hands on his head and moved away from the piloting station. Apparently, that wasn't good enough. The captain of the unit struck Jay behind his knee with the butt of his gun. His leg buckled and he was forced to the ground. Jay gritted his teeth on a grunt of pain as he collided with the floor. Bryce, at least, wasn't struck as he copied Jay's position.

Despite his knees throbbing from the rough collision with the metal, Jay still attempted to be pleasant.

"Any reason why we've been boarded?"

"We've done nothing," Bryce announced, his eyes on the captain.

Jay wanted to slap a hand to his forehead. Bryce was supposed to be distancing himself from Jay, not implying an association. Jay had to think fast.

"The guy's right," Jay hurried to add. "We were only leaving Vicente to share a few drinks, maybe a bed." He gave them a wry smile. "But this wasn't the weekend getaway I'd planned for him."

He's just an innocent fling, Jay was trying to convey. *He's not a thief or an accessory.*

Jay needed IA to dismiss Bryce and put him under witness protection. They wouldn't do that if they thought Bryce was a criminal. Jay hoped the captain would work it out and keep Bryce from accidentally incriminating himself. The captain didn't respond to them. He tilted his head in a motion implying that he was receiving orders through a communicator. A few seconds later he was gesturing for one of his agents to grab Bryce and pull him to his feet. The captain then did the same with Jay.

Jay grimaced as his arms were yanked behind his back and cuffed. The metal bit into his skin and made him want to jerk away, but he resisted the urge. Bryce was restrained as well and the agents marched them off the ship and into the cargo hold. Jay only had a moment to glance around. The captain set a brutal pace and shoved a firm hand between Jay's shoulders to keep him moving. Jay pressed his lips together, refusing to snap anything argumentative and make the situation worse.

He did get concerned when he was led in the opposite direction to Bryce. He tried to look over his shoulder but was shoved in the back again.

"Keep moving," the captain ordered.

Jay didn't like the separation, but he hoped Bryce was smart enough to follow his advice and keep himself out of trouble. The walk through the corridors of the ship took a good five minutes and ended with him being shoved into a containment cell. It had a hard bed, a toilet and nothing else. The link between his cuffs was deactivated, allowing him to move his arms in front of him again. The bracelets were still present and just waiting to be reactivated.

Wonderful, Jay thought.

He hoped Bryce was getting a more hospitable welcome and would be released soon. The waiter didn't deserve to be on IA's bad side just because he'd been captured on the wrong ship at the wrong time. Of course, Jay didn't deserve to be there either, but life was rarely fair. He might not be responsible for what had happened to the Qui, but he was a criminal all the same. The IA wouldn't be letting him go.

Sighing, Jay took a seat on the bed. They'd come to get him soon, and the questioning would be intense and drawn out. He'd withstood an Intelligence Agency interrogation before, and while it had been during a time Jay wished he could forget, he'd proven his innocence then and he'd do it again now. Jay just had to keep his answers simple and to the point, and not let them intimidate him.

It meant he needed to look at ease.

Shifting to spread out on the bed, Jay put his back to the wall, crossed his feet at the ankles and his arms over his chest. It was a shame he'd lost his hat to the dumpster on Vicente. He would have liked to tip it down over his eyes. He would also have loved a shower to clean off the stink and grime of trash, but his cleanliness wasn't an IA priority.

There was nothing to occupy his thoughts and Jay's mind turned to Bryce. *How is he faring? Is he in an interrogation right now? Did he listen to my advice or is he digging himself a deep hole?*

Jay told himself not to give a damn and to only think about himself, but it was hard. Somewhere between flirting on the moon and trading eye-rolls over annoying customers, Jay had started to like Bryce. It was a feeling made worse after having protected him from the explosion. It was an ingrained instinct to look out for someone he'd saved. He wished he could stop giving a damn and live up to the image he portrayed.

Jaybird was supposed to be an arrogant, uncaring, selfish asshole, but Jay had never been so heartless.

He tried to force his worry for Bryce from his mind, clearing his head and feigning relaxation to any IA agents who might be watching him. He whistled loud, annoying tunes for something to do and smacked his hand against the wall in a counter beat to keep himself occupied. It was as much a distraction as it was an attempt to look unconcerned with the situation.

He was almost relieved when his handcuffs reactivated after about an hour. He was running out of songs to whistle. Jay lifted his hands, observing the thin but unbreakable red energy link. The door opened and a new agent was revealed. His voice was gruff as he demanded, "On your feet."

Briefly, Jay debated arguing or refusing, but he decided that behaving would be better for him in the long run. He stood, taking a place in the center of the room.

"Step outside your cell."

Jay followed the next command. There was another agent in the hallway and they bracketed him on either side. They had energy guns just waiting to be used if he attempted to escape. Jay let them lead him through a dozen twists and turns. If they were trying to confuse him, it wasn't working. Jay was good at memorizing layouts and he already had a mental map from his ship to his containment cell and now to wherever they were going. He doubted he'd have the chance to use the information to launch an escape, but it was reassuring to know that he could, if given the opportunity.

Eventually, they stopped at a gray door that almost blended in with the wall. One of the agents pressed a hidden keypad and the door slid back to reveal a small room. It had a metal table and two chairs bolted to the floor, but no other furnishings. Jay was directed to sit in the chair facing the door. He obeyed, and once he was seated, they locked the door and left him alone.

Jay looked around curiously. *Why aren't they chaining me to the furniture?* If it weren't for his manacles, this could almost be considered a friendly chat. Jay tapped his fingers against the table. *What's their game?*

There wasn't a clock in the room, but Jay had a good internal watch. It hadn't been longer than two minutes before the door unlocked and opened. A man with graying hair, sharp eyes and a generic, easily forgettable face stepped inside. He shut the door before taking a seat opposite Jay. He had a hand-held datascreen, which he placed on the table. The screen was blank but the agent soon started typing. Information flooded the screen and the man ignored Jay to swipe through it.

"Jay, also known as Jaybird," he finally said.

Reports and images were selected and dismissed. Each one had a picture of Jay's winking mugshot in the corner. It was IA's dossier on his criminal activity.

"Wanted for a host of crimes across the galaxy," the agent continued. "Petty thievery, public nuisance and public indecency…" The agent raised his eyes to hold

Jay's. "And implicated in a dozen high-scale heists of jewelry, gold and priceless artifacts."

Jay kept his face blank and his lips sealed. He'd been implicated but never charged, and as long as he said nothing incriminating, it would stay that way. Yet the agent didn't push him on the subject. He changed it.

"But, more importantly to us..."

The agent tapped the upper right corner of the datascreen and turned it. He pushed it across the table toward him. Jay glanced down instinctively and gritted his teeth at the photo of himself — young and bright-eyed — from what felt like a lifetime ago.

"The honorably discharged Major Heath Chapman, a specialist in stealth and extraction."

Looking back at the agent, Jay remained silent. The man pulled the device back and moved through a different set of information, this time with Jay's service photo in the upper corner of the screen.

"You were a highly decorated officer, one of the finest operatives trained in the last decade." He looked back at Jay. "It's a shame you turned your talents to crime, Major."

"I was discharged," Jay said, glaring at the man. "I don't have a rank anymore."

"That's where we might disagree." The agent turned off the datascreen and put it to the side. He rested his elbows on the table and steepled his fingers. "We know of the warrants out for your arrest, Major, but we also know that you witnessed Zanik Taziv's kidnapping."

Jay frowned. "I don't see how those two things fit together."

"The Kada'rah orchestrated the kidnapping that you witnessed," the agent said bluntly.

Jay's stiffened. The Kada'rah was a violent and power-hungry criminal syndicate. They were ruthless and controlled a large portion of Asam. It was no surprise that they wanted to gain influence over the moons too.

"We have known of the threat to the Taziv family for some time," the agent explained. "The youngest son was the easiest target for the Kada'rah. We are appealing to his father to let us handle the safe return of Zanik. We want this resolved peacefully."

Jay narrowed his eyes. "Why would the IA care about the kidnapped son of a Qui who ignores galactic laws?" Jay's smile was ironic. "Or do you just want the Taziv family in your pocket rather than the Kada'rah's?"

"Major Chapman..." The agent remained calm and composed. "There is a fine balance maintained on those moons. It is a balance that benefits not only the criminals but IA too. We do not want to see it disturbed."

Jay didn't like where this was going. The agent's voice was too smooth and his information too freely given.

"What does this have to do with *me*?" he asked suspiciously.

"You are a specialist in stealth and extraction, a decorated soldier trained to work on almost every planetary terrain." His words were offered as facts as opposed to honeyed praise. "You are also a man who has spent the last five years becoming familiar with the more gray and illegal areas of society." The agent held Jay's gaze. "There are many IA operatives positioned across Asam and its moons, but removing them to work on this would endanger their lives and their missions.

There are no soldiers of your skill-set nearby who are available and enlisted — "

"Hold on," Jay interrupted, holding up his hands in the universal symbol for 'stop'. "You're trying to recruit me into a rescue mission?"

The agent picked up the datascreen once more and pulled up a new piece of information.

"Zanik is an innocent civilian in the hands of an organization known for torture." He showed a picture to Jay, giving him a good look at the young, smiling Qui. "The Intelligence Agency is offering to deactivate and dismiss all the outstanding warrants for your arrest if you accept this mission and reenlist for the time needed to complete it."

Jay slumped in his seat, feeling shocked. "You'll wipe my slate clean if I help rescue a Qui?"

"Yes," the agent answered.

But it just can't be that simple, can it?

Then again, going up against the Kada'rah would make most people run away with their tails between their legs. But Jay had run dozens of missions in active warzones. A criminal syndicate might be cruel and vindictive, but they couldn't take out an entire squadron in one hit. They couldn't do any worse than what had already been done to him — but Jay shut the door firmly on those unwanted memories.

There was a good reason that he'd ripped himself free from the Universal Collective and their Armed Forces Division. He couldn't trust the UCAFD and he'd wanted nothing more to do with them. It was why he'd thrown himself into the life of Jaybird. He'd been discharged, free to do what he wanted with his life.

Now how the tables have turned.

IA could be just as bad as the UCAFD, but what were his choices? Reenlist and lose any outstanding warrants or take his chances with whatever authorities the IA turned him over to? And what if they were telling the truth about not having a soldier nearby who could do what they needed?

Jay's gaze fell to the smiling face of Zanik, and his thoughts soon turned to Bryce. The waiter hadn't wanted anything to happen to the Qui. Could he really leave Zanik to the mercy of the Kada'rah? And what about Bryce? What was the IA going to do with him?

"What about the person I was with?" Jay asked. "Bryce, the waiter from the diner... What's happening to him?"

The agent raised a single surprised eyebrow. "He's not your concern."

"He damn well is," Jay argued. "Bryce is innocent and I want him kept free of any retaliation from the Kada'rah."

Narrowing his eyes, the agent studied Jay. It seemed to take an age before he admitted, "We've already made arrangements to hide his identity. He's not your concern, as he won't be returning to Vicente. You helped him remain undiscovered, and we will keep it that way."

Jay relaxed. He felt better knowing that Bryce would escape this mess in one piece.

"Now, will you agree to our terms, Major Chapman?"

Jay debated it a few moments more. He didn't want to enlist again, didn't want to go on another mission, but he was low on options. An unpleasant future awaited him if he declined. Freedom and the chance to start afresh beckoned if he accepted.

"I'm only bound to serve for as long as the mission takes?" Jay asked, still feeling wary.

"Yes," the agent agreed, his expression already filled with triumph.

He pulled up a service contract on the datascreen and pushed it toward Jay. Reading it through, Jay was impressed at how quickly they'd drawn it up. It was a simple agreement, free of fine print or loopholes. It specified that he would work with an IA agent familiar with the syndicate who had experience in the field. Jay didn't doubt that the agent would keep a sharp eye on him to make sure he played his role. The agency wouldn't trust Jay to stick to his word. He might be a thief with a useful past, but Jay had been a soldier for most of his life and the brotherhood and respect for those who served on the front lines never went away. Whoever they teamed him up with, Jay would fight them to his last breath.

Pressing his finger to the screen, Jay didn't second-guess as he signed on the bottom line. He sat back with heavy limbs. He was a soldier once more.

The datascreen was taken from him and the agent stood. He pressed a button on his belt and the chain of Jay's handcuffs deactivated. The cuffs followed it, opening and falling onto the table. Jay rubbed his wrists.

"You will be taken to your quarters, where you can shower and change. You will meet Commander Willis and Agent Fox for a debriefing in one hour. Understood, Major Chapman?"

Rising to stand, Jay gave a small, ironic smile. His voice was a light drawl, as opposed to the crisp agreement expected from a subordinate. "Yes, sir."

The agent didn't complain. He turned on his heel and left the room. He spoke briefly to the man outside before walking down the corridor. Jay made his way over to the waiting agent.

"If you'll follow me, sir," he said. "I will take you to your quarters."

Jay went without protest, following placidly behind a man who was now his subordinate. The routine of command structures and rank floated back over him like a long-forgotten dream. His walk shifted automatically, changing from a lazy, careless slump to straight-backed and sharp. He might have thrown himself into being Jay for five years, but he'd been a soldier for a decade before that, and some habits died hard.

When they reached the sleeping quarters he'd been given, he dismissed the agent. Jay ignored the bedroom to head for the bathroom. He stripped off his clothes and stepped into the shower. The hot water pounded down his shoulders as he washed off the grime from the dumpster. His mind drifted as he thought about what he was getting himself into. The Kada'rah wasn't an enemy anyone wanted to make. He hoped Agent Fox truly was an expert on the syndicate and knew better than to be foolish. Fox was a member of IA — a spy, by all accounts. He should be smart enough to follow Jay's judgment out in the field. It would be tough and dangerous, but if they succeeded in rescuing Zanik, Fox would have a gold star on his record and Jay would have a clean slate and the gratitude of Hezon Taziv.

The thought made Jay grin as he turned off the water and toweled himself dry. He'd never squander being free and in the favor of a rich and powerful family.

Wrapping the towel around his waist, Jay stepped into the main room. It was an interesting mix of emotions to find the brown and gray UCAFD uniform waiting for him on the bed. He supposed the IA had clothing on hand for every occasion that their agents might need. It didn't mean Jay's hands weren't heavy and his mind filled with memories as he pulled on each familiar layer.

When he'd finished and looked at himself in the mirror, it felt like he was being sent back in time, though his haircut wasn't standard issue and the clothing a tad big. It didn't designate him as a major, but it still felt like his old uniform. It was like being back there, about to walk into a new battle just because his commander had given an order. Jay swallowed and looked away. He could hear plasma gunfire, feel blood slick under his fingers and remember the cries of the men he'd trained with, fought with and formed friendships with. The memories were loud in his head, impossible to block out. He was grateful when a knock came on the door, jerking him from his thoughts.

"Come," he forced out, his voice rough.

The door opened. This time it was a female agent. "I'm here to take you to Commander Willis, sir."

Jay nodded and gave the room a quick glance, making sure he had forgotten nothing. Assured he was as presentable as he could be, Jay followed the agent out of the room and down a new set of hallways. It was a silent affair, with nothing but the echoing of their feet on the metal floors for sound. It gave Jay too much time to think.

How would he handle being in the field again? What orders would IA have for him? The UCAFD had a rhythm and structure that Jay knew. He had once been able to stretch their orders to the breaking point without reprisal. He'd known his men and who to trust on the battlefield. This was new territory, and although he could slide into his old skin with more ease than he'd ever had as Jaybird the thief, this was different enough to leave him tense. He cracked his knuckles — an old habit he'd picked up from a fellow major — to reduce some of his nerves. He was grateful to reach the briefing room and have something new to focus on.

The agent knocked on the door and, once she'd received permission, she opened it for Jay to walk through. The room was spacious, with a large table capable of fitting six people, though there was only one man present. He stood beside the table, wearing a dress uniform that defined his rank as commander. There was a datascreen in his hand and two others on the table. The commander paused his perusal of the information to give his attention to Jay. He itched to salute, but quelled the urge.

"Major." He directed him toward a chair. "Take a seat. We're waiting for Agent Fox."

The irony of the situation wasn't lost on Jay. Two hours ago, he had been a criminal waiting to be charged and jailed. Now he was an officer enjoying the respect and courtesy of his rank. It was as if the last five years had never happened.

Jay smiled wryly and murmured a half-hearted "Yes, sir."

He took the nearest chair facing the door, wanting to observe Agent Fox when he arrived. Jay looked over the commander in the meantime. He'd never heard of Commander Willis, but that meant nothing when dealing with the IA. The man was older than Jay, with shrewd eyes and long-healed burns on his neck and throat. It was obviously a wound sustained in battle from being too near an energy blast. A single war wound wasn't enough to allow him to trust a man, but Jay had found that those who'd served and suffered in battle were more critical and careful of the missions they sent their soldiers on. They didn't want others to suffer the way they had. It boosted Jay's confidence, and when he heard a knock on the door announcing Agent Fox, he felt ready for anything.

His thoughts changed the moment the agent entered the room. He walked with sure footing and was dressed in the standard black attire of an IA agent. His black hair was slicked back and when his blue eyes caught Jay's, there was something uneasy in them. He was almost wincing and Jay could understand why.

"Agent Fox, Major Chapman," the commander remarked, a hint of amusement in his voice. "I believe you know one another."

Jay didn't glance at Commander Willis. He was too busy staring at *Bryce*, the waiter he'd thought was innocent of everything, the person he'd been trying to protect and the man who was an IA agent undercover on Vicente.

Jay hadn't expected the bite of betrayal to hit him as hard as it did.

Chapter Three

"Major Chapman," Bryce greeted.

Jay clenched his fists. The urge to punch him was strong. How much of this was a setup? How long had Bryce known who and what he was? Anger coursed through Jay and it made his greeting bitter and accusatory. "*Bryce.*"

Agent Fox's cheek twitched, the only sign of his discomfort.

"Tristan," he corrected.

Of course, his name was part of the lie.

Jay scoffed in disgust and looked away from him. Everything that had happened on Vicente had been a fabrication. Bryce — *no, Tristan* — had only been flirting with him to gather information and pass it on to the Intelligence Agency. No wonder they'd known he'd take their offer of reenlistment. Tristan had probably been the one to suggest it.

What a fool he'd been. The signs of Tristan's duplicity had always been there if he'd only paid attention, rather than letting slim hips, bright eyes and an attractive grin distract him.

"Agent Fox," Commander Willis said, his sharp tone drawing their attention. "Take a seat." Tristan instantly obeyed, sitting opposite Jay. The commander glanced between them. "I understand this is not what you expected, Major, but Agent Fox was doing his job on Vicente and I expect you both to do the same here."

Jay was still angry at the deception, but there was little he could do about it. He had to work with Tristan if he wanted to gain his freedom and complete his contract with IA. Everything that had happened on Vicente and the attraction he'd felt... It all had to be put aside. He was a soldier on a mission and Tristan was an agent following orders. There was nothing more to it.

He felt Tristan's gaze on him but refused to catch his blue eyes.

"Yes, sir," Jay acknowledged the commander's request.

A beat later, Tristan did the same. Commander Willis accepted their words and took a seat at the head of the table.

"As you know," he began, "the Kada'rah took Zanik Taziv."

He tapped on his datascreen and Tristan did the same, prompting Jay to open his own. It displayed a wealth of information on the syndicate and the Taziv family. Jay's lips twitched bitterly. How much of the information had Tristan collected while posing as Bryce?

"Agent Fox has been monitoring both the Taziv family and the movements of the Kada'rah," Commander Willis continued, confirming Jay's thoughts. "They've been expanding out from Asam and onto its moons over the last few years. The Taziv family was the obvious target for a kidnapping, but our intelligence hadn't indicated the syndicate planned to move against them."

"But now they've kidnapped Zanik," Jay stated.

"Which has forced our hand," Commander Willis agreed. "You may have been out of combat for the last few years, Major, but your records show you have the necessary skills to help us to extract Zanik."

"Right." Jay tapped his fingers against the table as he considered the situation. "Where are they holding him?"

"They have a compound in the foothills at the edge of the Carana Desert on Asam," Tristan answered. They locked eyes, and he held Jay's gaze without flinching. "We have reconnaissance photos and digitized models, but there are too many tunnels into the mountain to be certain of Zanik's exact location in the compound."

Jay located the images on the datascreen and accessed the 3D image of the compound. It spun slowly, allowing him to view all potential entry points. It had been years since Jay had last sat in a debriefing, but his training made it all second-nature. Jay ran through the options for extraction and what he would need to make them feasible.

He turned to the commander and asked, "How do we get onto the planet?"

"We have a few options," the commander answered. "But your ship will be the wisest choice."

It was subtle and shouldn't draw attention — but that was only one step in a longer plan. The spaceports of Asam were hours from the Carana Desert, and depending on how deep into the sands the compound was, they might need to hire either equines or sand jeeps.

"Right," Jay said, rubbing a hand over his jaw. "How do you want us to get there?"

The UCAFD preferred air drops, but IA wouldn't want such a frontal assault, not with only a two-man team. Jay's assumption proved correct as the commander explained the outline devised for the mission. It was him and Tristan, sneaking their way across the desert. Tristan chimed in with additional information, which Jay often disputed.

Commander Willis was intelligent, but he was a man who had obviously spent years commanding a ship, an officer more than a soldier. He focused on the big picture and the fastest way to achieve it. Tristan was a man of covert operations with no experience in war zones. He left no trace of his presence and stole information from behind enemy lines. He was used to working alone.

Jay had been a soldier on the front lines, used to working with a team and surviving through sheer grit, despite the horrific situations he had been thrown into. They all saw the problem with different eyes, and while their goal was the same, they argued on how best to get there. It took a half hour of discussion before a plan could be reached.

Tristan and Jay would fly down to Asam in Jay's ship the next morning. They would hire equines for the trek across the desert. Equines were slower than sand jeeps but would attract less attention. They would make their way to the Kada'rah compound, locate Zanik and get him to the extraction point.

It was a standard mission for Jay, until it turned to breaching the syndicate's walls. Normally, he would plan for an assault with the guarantee of some form of combat. Some of his men would fight, others would extract the prisoner. IA was different. That outcome was a worst-case scenario. They wanted Zanik found and removed as quietly as possible. Tristan's knowledge of the Kada'rah, combined with information from undercover operatives, would prove invaluable for sneaking in.

Personally, Jay believed they were being too optimistic. This would end in combat and explosions, he was certain, but until the time came, he'd let them dream optimistically.

When the briefing concluded, Commander Willis switched off the datascreen and turned to Jay.

"Thank you for your input, Major. Be prepared to begin your mission tomorrow morning." He gestured at the datascreen Jay still held. "Take it and familiarize yourself with the syndicate and terrain of Asam. You're dismissed."

Jay stood and gave a nod. "Sir."

He left without glancing at Tristan.

Unsurprisingly, there was an IA agent waiting to escort him to his quarters. The Intelligence Agency didn't trust him and Jay didn't trust them. Tristan was no doubt gaining a side mission—extract information from the Kada'rah systems and shoot Jay in the back of the head if he betrayed them. IA always had a mission inside a mission—like a cute waiter flirting with a potentially useful thief. Jay gritted his teeth. The sting from the lie persisted.

What had Tristan passed on to IA about him? How much more interesting would Jaybird have needed to be before 'Bryce' would have climbed into his bed? Would Tristan have slept with Zanik if they'd ordered him to? Had he already slept with the Qui?

Jay let out an irritated breath and tried to shrug off his thoughts. It didn't matter who the agent had sex with or whether his attraction to Jay was real. The only thing that mattered was completing the mission and getting the hell away from IA.

Jay was glad to reach his quarters and shut the door. He took a seat on the bed and turned on the datascreen. Jay tried to focus on the Kada'rah, yet despite his best efforts, thoughts of Tristan continued to linger. He kept comparing the smirking waiter with the stiff-backed agent with slicked-back hair. How much of Bryce had been real? Why couldn't he let it go?

But he knew why.

Bryce had been intriguing and fun. He'd even fantasized about flying Bryce to another planet for a weekend getaway. He hadn't planned to settle down with him or make Bryce his partner in crime — but Jay had liked Bryce, and now he had to let the other man go. Bryce was make-believe. Agent Tristan Fox was real. The man he'd been trying to know didn't exist.

He had to shake off his feelings. Nothing but the mission mattered. He'd ignore Tristan, rescue Zanik and leave IA behind.

Determined, Jay turned back to the datascreen and finally lost himself in reports. There was a large amount of information redacted, but Jay could read between the lines. IA had two undercover operatives working inside the Kada'rah's ranks. They were far enough from the compound that Jay and Tristan wouldn't run into them, but it was why they wanted to limit damage to the Kada'rah's forces. They wanted them intact so IA could continue to mine information from the syndicate.

Jay was so immersed that the last thing he expected was an interruption. The knock on his door prompted him to look up from the datascreen. He frowned. Who would want to see him?

"Come," Jay called.

He certainly hadn't expected it to be Tristan Fox.

The agent stepped into the room and shut the door. He turned to face Jay, standing with his back straight and his hands at his sides.

"We need to have a conversation," Tristan said, simple and to the point.

Jay raised his eyebrows. "Did Commander Willis recommend that?"

"No," Tristan answered. "But it's necessary if we're going to work together."

Locking the datascreen and putting it beside him, Jay wondered what Tristan planned to do. Just seeing the other man put Jay on edge and made his annoyance resurface.

"What do you want to talk about? Did you come to apologize? Then again, maybe you came to tell me that we didn't have sex because I didn't have enough information to warrant it?"

Tristan's jaw clenched, and he glared at Jay. It was the same expression Bryce had used to display, only made harsher by his styled hair and dark uniform.

"I don't sleep with my targets," Tristan said, his voice angry. "You flirted with me and I flirted back so I could determine your affiliation with the Kada'rah."

Jay stood. His frustration made it impossible to remain seated.

"And what would have happened if I'd had information?" He stalked forward until they were nose-to-nose. "What would Tristan Fox have done with me then?"

"I had a mission to complete and superiors to report to. I would have done what was necessary." He held Jay's gaze. "It's something I believe you can understand, Major Chapman."

The remark hit its intended target, and Jay had to look away. The words didn't erase all his anger at being

45

used and manipulated—but Tristan was right. Jay understood. He didn't like it, but Jay couldn't argue with a fellow soldier who was following orders.

"Look..." Tristan said, his voice softened. "I didn't know who you were until we arrived. They told me you were not a person of interest on Vicente and to disengage, so I did."

"And that's supposed to make things better?" Jay asked, looking back at him.

Tristan's fingers twitched at his side, a frustrated habit that both Bryce and Tristan shared.

"I am trying to explain my part in our association," Tristan said.

Jay laughed wryly. "An IA agent being candid with me? Will wonders never cease?"

"Would you prefer I said nothing?" Tristan snapped. "Allow this"—he gestured between them—"to fester?"

"And what is *this*?" Jay demanded. He didn't know what he wanted, but the urge to shove the other man was strong. "A spy doing his job?"

"No, Major Chapman, that's not what's between us."

Tristan had barely finished speaking before he was kissing him. Jay's eyes widened with surprise. Tristan brought his hands to Jay's shoulders then slid them up his neck, tugging him closer. Instinctively, Jay kissed him back. He put his hands on the man's waist, just like he'd imagined doing for weeks. The kiss soon became a battle of mouths. Tristan bit Jay's bottom lip, tugging and sucking it before diving back in for more. The kiss was rough with need and yearning, just like he'd pictured kissing Bryce would be—only this wasn't Bryce. This was a spy with as many missions under his belt as Heath Chapman had.

The reminder forced Jay to tear his mouth away from the agent. He was panting and so was Tristan. The guy's blue eyes were darker than usual, but he was seemingly analyzing Jay's reaction.

Right now, all Jay felt was confusion, arousal and shock.

"What the hell?" he asked. "Are you trying to ensure my loyalty or something?"

Tristan barked out a laugh.

"No, Major, I told you. I don't sleep with my marks. I also doubt spending the night together would change how much I can trust you." He trailed his fingers over Jay's neck in teasing invitation. "But as of tomorrow, we will be on a mission together." Tristan almost smiled. "I think it would be better if we got this out of our systems before working in such close quarters, don't you?"

The evidence was obvious, yet Jay had trouble believing it.

"Your attraction to me was real?"

"Yes, it was," Tristan admitted. "I couldn't act on it before and we can't let it compromise us once the mission begins." He shrugged. "But right now? We have a narrow window of opportunity."

The offer was tempting. It was what he'd wanted for weeks. When else would he get the chance? He'd never planned for anything other than meaningless sex with Bryce. Why did it have to be different with Tristan?

And as Tristan had said, it might even help. There was desire from weeks of flirtation and anger from the last few hours. Combining that with the strain of current events and objectives?

We could both use an outlet.

Decision made, Jay cupped Tristan's neck and pulled him in for another kiss. Their lips caught and

Tristan started encouraging him backward and toward the bed. Jay moved without protest.

Tristan kissed as if there was a battle to be won and Jay refused to go down without a fight. The kiss was harsh, but Jay loved the sharpness. He slid his fingers through Tristan's hair, tugging at the strands. Tristan nipped at Jay's lower lip in retaliation, making Jay groaned with desire.

They only broke apart when Jay's legs hit the bed. Tristan smirked, looking pleased with himself.

"I'm glad we're in agreement, Major."

Tristan went to kiss him, but Jay held him back. The man frowned.

"Jay," he told Tristan. "It's not 'Major' or 'Heath'. When you're sharing my bed, it's Jay."

The agent shrugged. "Fine."

He kissed Jay again while his hands went to the buttons of Jay's uniform. He responded by gripping the smooth material of Tristan's shirt and trying to tug it over his head. Tristan broke the kiss with a chuckle before pushing his hands away and standing back.

"Perhaps we should each undress ourselves," Tristan remarked.

Tristan stepped over to the small table in Jay's quarters. He started removing a small arsenal of hidden weapons. They were all standard items, but each one was expertly hidden or stitched into his clothes.

It made sense that an IA agent would never be unarmed, even on an IA ship. IA was notoriously paranoid. Jay shook his head and pulled off his clothing. He didn't have a weapon on him and maybe he should have felt vulnerable, but if IA wanted him dead, they would already have killed him.

Jay stripped down to his pants and kicked off his shoes and socks. He glanced over to find Tristan folding his shirt onto the nearby chair. Stripping separately could have spoiled the mood, but one look at Tristan's uncovered back and arched spine made Jay's cock harden and his hands tingle with the need to touch. Tristan was gorgeous. He had the occasional freckle or mole marring his skin and Jay wanted to trail his lips over them. There were three scars Jay could see, looking like they were from knife wounds, but nothing else.

Jay had more scars than Tristan. His body showed his near-misses and hardships for his every lover to see. His wounds were a testament of survival and he was proud of them. Tristan seemed to like what he saw too, as his cock was still hard as he looked Jay up and down.

Their bodies, like their lives, were polar opposites. Tristan was slim and pale. He was built for fast, efficient strikes meant to disable and capture. Jay was tan from years under the sun, with larger muscles gained from heavy lifting and intense physical training. Jay might not have been following the training routine of a soldier for the past few years, but he still worked hard to maintain his strength and resilience.

Tristan stepped toward him. He explored Jay's chest with his hands while he caught his mouth in another kiss. Jay ran his hands down Tristan's sides, enjoying the smooth warm skin and the hint of raised flesh. Where had the scar along his ribs come from?

Tristan sought out every blemish on Jay's skin on the way down to his pants. He flicked open the button and zip with ease before reaching inside. Jay broke the kiss to groan as Tristan cupped his hardening length and gave it a slow stroke.

Damn, that feels good.

Jay turned his attention to the agent's pants, getting them undone and open. When he emcircled Tristan's arousal with his fist, the agent tipped his head forward and panted against Jay's jaw. The angle and position were awkward, but they made do.

Soon, Tristan apparently got tired of the exploration. He brushed his lips over Jay's cheek before moving to his ear.

"You've offered to give me a ride for weeks, Jay. Going to live up to your word?"

Jay bit down on a groan, making it come out more like a grunt. He brought his free hand to the back of Tristan's neck and tugged him in for another kiss. The press of their mouths was quick to deepen. They tangled their tongues and Tristan removed his hand from Jay's pants. He scraped his nails along Jay's back, and he arched and hissed.

Palming each other had been fun, but Tristan had made a challenge, and Jay was taking it.

Jay slipped his hand from Tristan's pants and broke the kiss. Jay started unbuckling his pants and Tristan kicked off his own. Both pair landed on the floor and the men climbed onto the bed. Jay touched Tristan's upper arm, planning to guide him farther up the bed, but Tristan shifted unexpectedly. He slid toward the headboard, apparently having the same idea as Jay. He cupped Jay's neck and tugged him into another kiss. Jay ended up crouched over Tristan, kneeling between his legs and trying to keep up with Tristan's mouth.

It wasn't what he'd expected, but Bryce had made a habit of surprising him. It seemed Tristan was no different.

When Tristan's right leg hooked over his hip, dragging Jay down until their pelvises came together, the kiss broke. Tristan moaned softly while Jay pulled in a harsh breath. They started to rock their hips together, desperate for friction.

Jay pressed his lips to Tristan's neck, mouthing at the skin. Tristan tilted his neck into the touch, letting out a small hiss of pleasure as he tangled his fingers in Jay's hair. Jay moved from Tristan's neck to his collarbones, then to his chest. He liked the spot where Tristan's neck met his shoulder, and a small nibble on the skin made Tristan shiver all over.

Looking up at him, Jay admired the sight. His cheeks were flushed and his eyes were half-lidded. His hair had mussed and broken from its slicked-back state, and he almost looked like Bryce. Moving farther down Tristan's chest, he bypassed his dark nipples and focused instead on the knife wound.

Who did Tristan Fox double-cross to earn that?

But Tristan was seemingly growing impatient. He tugged firmly at Jay's hair, making him lift his lips.

"I thought you promised me a ride," Tristan said.

"I like the scenic route," Jay quipped.

Tristan rolled his eyes. "I prefer to get to the main event. We have a mission in only a handful of hours."

The reminder was like a bucket of cold water.

"Right," Jay muttered.

Tristan shifted and grabbed something from near the pillows. He passed it to Jay, who blinked.

How the hell did lube end up on my bed?

"Where did you get that?"

"I brought it with me," Tristan said. "I couldn't guarantee you would have any with you."

"Where did you hide it?" Jay asked, looking Tristan up and down. "You were naked. You didn't have pockets." His eyes dropped to Tristan's ass. "Unless you—"

"Don't be ridiculous," Tristan muttered, sounding impatient, "and stop wasting time."

He pushed Jay's shoulder, forcing him to back away and kneel by Tristan's feet. The moment he had the room, Tristan shifted onto his hands and knees, waiting for Jay to prepare him. That position was a little too cold and clinical for Jay's tastes. Sex was meant to be fun. He supposed that was what he got for sleeping with an IA agent whose mind was already half on the mission they'd share in the morning.

Uncapping the vial and pouring some lube onto his fingers, Jay mourned the lack of extended foreplay or the ability to watch Tristan's face crest with pleasure as he pressed inside him. Jay always liked seeing his partners enjoy themselves — but he wasn't about to complain about the specifics when he had a throbbing cock and Tristan in his bed.

Warming the lubricant between his fingers, Jay shifted into place and spread Tristan's ass cheeks. Tristan dropped down farther to lie on his arms, giving Jay a better angle to work. Jay grinned and pressed his first finger to the other man's entrance. He ran the pad over the tight pucker and heard Tristan let out a soft breath. The agent's muscles relaxed.

He slipped his first finger inside. Tristan was tight, but it wouldn't be hard to fix that. Jay took his time, pressing in, rotating it and pulling out. He brought his mouth to Tristan's lower back, scraping his teeth over the skin and sucking it gently. Tristan shuddered and made noises of encouragement.

Jay continued to spread him wide, thrusting a second finger inside and curling them as he searched for Tristan's prostate. When he found it, Tristan's breath punched out of him in a groan. He arched, even as he pressed back against Jay's fingers. The agent's knuckles were white as he clenched the bedding.

Jay's arousal throbbed with want, desperate to be touched and stimulated. He wanted to stroke himself — but he also wanted get inside Tristan. The time for teasing had passed.

He gave Tristan's prostate a final brush before pulling his fingers out. His voice was rough as he asked, "Ready?"

"*Yes*," Tristan gritted out in a tone filled with frustration and yearning.

Jay smirked. He poured a little more lube onto his hand before stroking and coating his erection. He squeezed behind the head and teased himself. It felt so good, and the sight in front of him was just as pleasurable. Tristan was spread before him, his hole twitching and waiting to be speared by Jay. His skin was beaded with sweat and Tristan's cock hung hard and heavy between his thighs.

What a beautiful image.

Taking his position behind Tristan, Jay shifted the agent's hips to the perfect angle. He took his rock-hard member in hand and brushed Tristan's entrance. Tristan trembled with need.

When Jay pushed inside, they both moaned. Tristan's muscles clenched around him, seeming to hug Jay's shaft and drag it deeper. The heat and tightness caused Jay to close his eyes. He panted, but Tristan's breaths came in hitched groans. It seemed to take both forever and no time at all before Jay was completely sheathed. He took a moment to catch his breath, leaning over Tristan's sweat-dampened back.

Tristan was the first to react by pushing his hips back against Jay. He demanded, "Move."

Jay laughed but complied. He grasped Tristan's hips and pulled out slowly before rocking back in. They both moaned. Tristan clenched and unclenched the sheets, but he didn't lie passive. He started to rock his hips back against Jay's thrusts. They established a rhythm that found them groaning on every second breath. When Jay angled himself to strike Tristan's prostate, Tristan's voice broke on a curse. He arched his body as if an electric current had shot through it.

After that, Jay made sure to never miss.

It was a heady, intense pace, with nothing but the tang of sweat on his tongue as Jay mouthed at Tristan's skin. The sounds of their pleasure and the rocking of the bed were loud. Jay could almost forget he wasn't on his ship. He could almost pretend it was his intriguing waiter who had finally succumbed to his charms. But the chemical cleanliness of military bedding lingered in the air and disrupted the fantasy. The man beneath him had scars that a waiter would most likely never possess and a personality that came from a life of orders, secrets and ranks.

Remembering the lie that had brought him here, Jay clenched his teeth and shut his eyes, making his thrusts even more harsh. He pushed into Tristan sharply, but the agent only moaned for more.

"Harder," Tristan gasped. "Put some effort into it."

Jay barked a surprised laugh and his thrusts faltered. He opened his eyes and grinned down at the man.

"So full of surprises," he replied.

If Tristan planned to respond, Jay silenced him by increasing his speed and intensity. His strikes became brutal as he pushed them closer to the peak.

Tristan rolled into each movement. His cheek was pressed to the bedding, his lips parting in silent bliss. Jay leaned forward on a whim and nipped at the skin of Tristan's shoulder. The agent opened lust-glazed eyes. He looked more like Bryce than Tristan, and he was utterly gorgeous. Jay could have spent hours admiring him, but Tristan was definitely impatient. He clenched his muscles around Jay's cock, causing him to moan.

"Don't slow down," Tristan demanded with a voice wrecked with pleasure.

Tristan snuck a hand beneath his stomach to fist himself. He squeezed his eyes shut and his moans came unbidden. The sounds he made were enough to drive a man wild, causing Jay's thrusts to become even more frantic. He closed his eyes and focused on the feel and sounds of Tristan underneath him. His climax was approaching and Tristan obviously wasn't far behind.

Tristan was gasping underneath him, the pitch and frequency of his groans increasing. He was close. Jay didn't think as he attacked the spot where Tristan's neck met his shoulder and latched on. He sucked before biting down hard enough to leave a mark, maybe even a bruise. Tristan went stiff against Jay, his breath catching before he let out a blissful cry. His body jerked and his muscles contracted as he came. The feel of Tristan's orgasm brought Jay right to the edge. He grabbed Tristan's hips and thrust rapidly, chasing his own pleasure. It hit him like a wave, slamming into him and punching the breath from his lungs. Jay moaned against Tristan's skin.

Damn. What a ride.

He felt the bliss from good sex in every muscle. He pulled out of Tristan but was careful to put space between them as he lay on the mattress and panted. Tristan remained beside him, collecting his breath. It was long enough that Jay wondered, *What now?*

But Jay didn't have long to debate the question, as Tristan shifted and rolled off the mattress. He moved straight to the bathroom without a word or backward glance. He only paused long enough to grab his clothes before he shut the door.

Jay lingered on the bed, waiting to see what would happen. In the end, he felt too unsettled to stay there. He climbed from the mattress and pulled on his pants. It was strange. He was normally the one yanking on his clothes and parting with a kiss and a wink before anyone could see him. It was odd to be on the opposite side of the equation.

But it was a good thing, wasn't it? There would be no pillow talk, no awkward questions, no emotional attachments.

He'd offered meaningless sex—and so had Tristan. Jay would still be leaving once Zanik was rescued, and Tristan would go back to undercover work for IA. A one-night stand didn't make a bit of difference.

After stripping the bed, he located some spare sheets and remade it before he took a seat back on the mattress with his datascreen.

Tristan stepped back into the room less than ten minutes later. The agent's hair was perfect once more and his skin was no longer flushed. Tristan glanced at Jay but soon focused on sliding his weapons back into their various hiding places. He straightened his shirt when he'd finished, and turned to Jay. He was the perfect professional once more.

"I hope we will now be able to work together comfortably, Major Chapman."

Jay found his lip twitching in both amusement and incredulity. Tristan was so matter-of-fact. It was impressive how well he'd played the role of Bryce, if this was his normal personality. It was also impressive how optimistic IA trained their agents to be.

Jay's resentment and anger over the lie had faded, but he doubted a brief time in bed had solved all their problems. His attraction to Tristan hadn't disappeared, and the memory of the agent moaning beneath him wouldn't go away overnight. But if Tristan wanted to pretend it was swept under the rug, Jay could do the same.

"I don't think we'll have a problem, Agent Fox."

Tristan nearly smiled, but he was turning away before the expression could fully form. He left without another word.

It could have seemed impolite, but they weren't friends or true comrades. They had been thrown together by chance and unfortunate circumstances. Their mission would take less than a week to complete, then they would be out of each other's lives. Jay would be free from the weight of Major Chapman and back to the disreputable, thieving existence of Jaybird.

It will be easier that way.

Sighing, Jay tossed aside the datascreen and lay down on his back, staring at the ceiling. He thought about Tristan. The sex had been good.

When he closed his eyes, his mind replayed it — yet it was overlaid by the smirks and flirtations of an innocent waiter who'd made him laugh. Jay would miss visiting that diner on Vicente.

Jay sighed again and opened his eyes. His fury might be gone and his desire might have faded, but Jay's disappointment at losing Bryce still lingered.

Chapter Four

Jay woke early the next morning. He showered and shaved but was still wrapped in a towel when an IA agent knocked on his door to deliver his clothing for the mission. The outfit was comprised of thick black boots, dark brown pants with numerous pockets, a black shirt and a dark brown wrap. It was standard desert attire. The shawl he could drape over his body, shoulders and head to protect him from the whipping wind and sand.

Pulling on everything but the wrap, he stepped out of his room. He asked directions from the first agent he found and headed to the mess hall for breakfast. It was swarming with agents, but unlike the UCAFD, which would be loud and raucous, the spies were quiet. The few conversations were done in whispers so that no one could eavesdrop. Jay could feel everyone's eyes on him, even if they weren't obvious about it. Jay ate alone, and although he did skim the room, he didn't see Tristan.

When he returned to his quarters, Jay put on the shawl and looked around. There was nothing else

worth taking. He left the datascreen and his clothes —
IA could wash them or throw them out. He didn't care.

When Jay arrived at the docking bay, it was just
before their scheduled departure time. Tristan was
already there. His black hair was loose and falling in
soft curls once more and he had similar boots and wore
lighter-colored but otherwise identical pants to Jay's.
Instead of a shawl, he had a dark brown hooded wrap,
which sat more like a poncho or cape. When Tristan
shifted, Jay could see a brown shirt under it. A shemagh
was wrapped around Tristan's neck. It was a scarf-like
item that would protect his face and neck from sun and
sand in the desert .

They would fit right in on Asam.

There were a few agents in the docking bay doing
pre-mission tasks. A man stood by Jay's ship, ticking
items off a list. Figuring that was a good place to start,
Jay made his way over and ordered, "Report."

The agent looked over his shoulder and Jay
witnessed his internal struggle as he decided whether
or not to answer, but Jay was a major and outranked
him.

"I have placed all items on board that are relevant to
the mission. The ship is refueled and ready for flight,
sir."

Jay almost smiled. It must irritate them to take
orders from a criminal and to care for his ship as if it
were part of their fleet. A lesser man might have abused
that power, but not Jay. He didn't want IA angry with
him. He would check his ship for surveillance once they
rescued the Qui, then he hoped to be done with the lot
of them.

"Excellent," Jay replied.

"We'll leave immediately," Tristan added, appearing beside him.

Jay managed not to flinch. Tristan was very good at sneaking up on people.

He turned and caught Tristan's eyes. His gaze was expectant, as he was simply waiting for Jay to agree to his demand. There wasn't any reason to argue, but Jay wanted to needle Tristan. Their arguments had been fun back at the diner, and even in Jay's quarters the previous night they'd pushed one another, delighting in each reaction.

But that was then, and this was a mission. They had to be professional.

He couldn't resist making a grand, sweeping gesture with his arm toward the ship. "After you, Agent Fox."

Tristan's expression was unreadable. He looked Jay up and down but didn't say another word as he stepped onboard the ship. Jay followed behind him. The moment he was inside and the door was shut, he let out a soft breath of relief. He could feel the claustrophobic layers of 'Major Chapman' peeling off him. He wasn't dressed in a UCAFD uniform and once they left, no one would be calling him 'sir'. He could already taste freedom in the air.

They still needed to complete the mission, but the instinct to stand straight and fall into the chain of command was fading. This was his ship, and he wasn't Major Chapman here. He was doing a mission for IA, but it didn't mean he had to stop being the person he'd become—being Jaybird. He needed to be the lighthearted, devil-may-care Jay if he wanted to make it through without ugly memories resurfacing.

Making his way to the helm of the ship, Jay turned his attention back to the present instead of the past.

Tristan was already sitting in the co-pilot chair. Jay ignored the unfamiliar sight and sat down beside him. Jay booted up the engines and punched in the flight details.

"This part of Asam isn't fond of travelers," Tristan remarked.

Jay glanced at the agent. Tristan had leaned back and was reading the information on the screen with a frown. Jay grinned.

"This part of Asam is fond of swindling travelers and sending them out in the desert to die."

Tristan sent him an unimpressed glare. "That would be my point."

"You just have to know the right way around them," Jay said. "After all" — he winked — "they're fonder of a blackguard than a tourist."

"Which is the entire reason the Kada'rah have such a strong foothold on the planet," Tristan riposted, still scowling.

"I think that's unnecessarily harsh," Jay remarked. He looked back at the screen, waiting for clearance to exit the docking bay. "Maybe they just like a good bit of fun."

He could feel Tristan's eyes on him but didn't turn to look.

"I know who you are, Major Chapman," Tristan said. "Why do you continue to act like Jaybird the thief?"

Jay kept himself busy with the ship.

"Why do you think it's an act?"

"It's part of my job to know the difference."

"That doesn't mean you're always right."

Outwardly, Jay kept himself relaxed and at ease, but inside he felt uncomfortable. Tristan's eyes were sharp and he was analyzing Jay like he was a puzzle. Jay didn't want the agent to solve him.

"It doesn't," Tristan finally agreed. "I didn't pick you for a soldier when we first met, but I knew you weren't the carefree blackguard you pretend to be."

The intensity of his gaze reminded Jay of the previous night. Tristan saw people as mysteries to solve and discard. He'd done the same to Jay. They'd had sex, then he'd turned away and pulled on the role of an agent without a backward glance. He'd dismissed their physical attraction as if it were no longer relevant.

Jay understood, to some degree. Tristan needed to separate himself from his emotions to survive and function as an undercover agent. Jay needed a similar mindset when in the field. Injury and feelings all had to be pushed aside for the sake of completing the mission. It was only when he was back on the base that he could process them. When Jay had left the UCAFD, he'd taken a similar approach to his life and his past. The soldier was something he put to the side, and the thief was something he picked up to keep him focused and busy. Maybe Jaybird was a role, but it didn't mean Jay wanted to admit that to Tristan.

He didn't want the man to learn why he'd become Jaybird.

It left Jay unsure of what to say, and when he spoke, he surprised himself with his honesty.

"I left the UCAFD five years ago, Tristan. You think Jaybird is an act? Well, so is Major Chapman. If we want to work together successfully, you need to understand that. You also need to call me Jay."

Tristan's eyebrows rose. "Is that so?"

"Take it or leave it, Tristan," Jay said, catching and holding his gaze. "But things will be easier and more amicable if you go along with my request."

"I don't care what name you choose," Tristan replied. "I just want to see our mission succeed."

"Good," Jay answered.

He was relieved they'd managed an agreement without descending into a verbal battle. It had been their main form of communication back at the diner, but this boded well for them working together.

Maybe the sex really did take the edge off.

A crackle from the communicators giving them approval for their departure focused Jay's attention. He raised the ship off the deck and guided it to the bay doors. It didn't take long for the cargo bay to clear, allowing him to finally exit the IA craft. Jay sighed with relief as he looked at the blanket of stars before him. Asam and its moons were in the distance, looking beautiful and peaceful. In moments like this, Jay could appreciate why some people devoted their lives to flying. Jay preferred to have his feet on the ground as he explored a new place, but staring out at the vastness of space? Jay loved that. He'd tasted the freedom of the universe, and he would forever crave the adventure that came from traveling through it.

"When we arrive on Asam," Tristan said, interrupting Jay's drifting thoughts and making him look at the agent, "will the people know you as Jaybird?"

Jay shook his head. "Never been down to that particular spaceport. And I'm not known in this part of the galaxy anyway."

Tristan nodded. "Then a simple cover of two thieves evading the authorities should suffice."

Jay eyed Tristan oddly. "You know thieves don't give that information away for free, don't you? We won't be advertising ourselves. Land the ship, grab the equines, head into the desert. The people we barter from aren't meant to remember us."

"Yes, I'm aware," Tristan answered, sounding irritated. "But people only forget you if you give them no cause for suspicion or alarm." His voice took on a lecturing tone, as if Jay were an underling on his first assignment. "Acting at odds with one another is the quickest way to be noticed by the enemy."

"Tips from a pro, huh?" Jay drawled, dry amusement coating his voice. "A spy's guide to turning tricks."

Tristan looked unamused by his turn of phrase, and Jay remembered his words from the previous night. *'I don't sleep with my targets.'* There had been frustration and offense in his voice. How many people assumed Tristan whored himself? How many people didn't believe him when Tristan said otherwise? Jay didn't want to be one of them. He wanted to smooth this over.

"A soldier acts more simply," Jay offered, sidestepping his faux pas. "Keep your head down and do your job. You're a man who wants to buy horses. That's all they need to see."

"The training is similar," Tristan agreed, the frost in his eyes thawing. "But where a soldier carries his training in every step, an IA agent must carry nothing but his guise."

Tristan suddenly smiled. His expression was innocent and his posture relaxed. He held out his hand in an open, easy gesture. It was all an act, but it was an impressive one. He looked even more naïve than Bryce.

"A waiter doesn't know what the price for an equine is, does he? Why, he's a swindle just waiting to happen." He bit his lip and widened his eyes, looking shy and hopeful. "Until some nice man spots him and offers aid, for this waiter has *such* a pretty face."

Jay huffed out a laugh and Tristan dropped the demure act to lean back in the chair, once more the calm, composed agent.

"You have to know the role before you can play it, Jay."

Jay nodded, still feeling amused. He could have held on to anger over the reminder of being tricked, but the more Jay thought about it and the longer he had to cool down, the more he accepted it. Jay was one of many, and Tristan hadn't been out to con him specifically. Hell, Tristan's abilities impressed him. Jay had met successful conmen who didn't have half as much talent as the agent.

He could respect Tristan. The man wanted to help people and protect the universe. Jay might not trust organizations anymore, but he could trust individual people. He had no choice *but* to trust Tristan. They were going on a mission together, and as a soldier, he had to believe that the man had his back.

It helped that he liked him, too.

The sex had softened the tension between them, but Tristan was still intelligent, funny and striking. The fact that he was an IA agent didn't put a damper on Jay's interest. It made him wonder who would win in a true fight. What it would be like to grapple on the ground with him? Would Tristan have enough tricks to pin him?

It was a shame they'd never find out.

"Okay," Jay said, shaking off his thoughts, "so, we're thieves." Switching the ship to autopilot, Jay turned in his seat to face Tristan, willing to play along with the agent's mission process. "Why are we evading the authorities?"

Tristan shifted in his own seat until they were knee-to-knee.

"Isn't that your area to draw from, Jaybird?" he asked with a grin.

Jay chuckled.

"All right. What are your skills? Why am I teaming up with a thief like you?" He looked the agent up and down but couldn't resist the tease, "It's that pretty face, isn't it?"

His remark made Tristan laugh. His expression wasn't as artless and open as Bryce the waiter's or as rigid as Tristan the agent's. It was reminiscent of the straightforward man who had come into Jay's quarters and cleared the air of lies and sexual tension.

It was like peeling away one strange and interesting layer after another, and damn it all, Jay liked it. He was just as intrigued by Tristan as he had been with Bryce — and that meant he had to be careful. This wasn't some fling. This was an IA agent. Their association and mission would end with the two of them on opposite sides.

Although, a part of Jay chimed in, *it doesn't mean you can't have some fun with him. It's a long mission and you're both adults. Who would it hurt?*

But, realistically, what were the odds that Tristan would be interested in another night with him? Why would either of them jeopardize the mission for another round of casual sex?

* * * *

It didn't take long to reach Asam and land the ship, but they had spent the time devising their façade. Tristan was the conman, his flash and smirk distracting everyone's attention. Jay would stand in the shadows, his nimble fingers stealing items of value from their oblivious audience. They had recently completed a large con and were hiding out while the heat died down. It was an easy role for Jay to play, and if Tristan wanted a backstory to better help him work the mission, Jay was willing to go along with it.

The starport they had chosen was one of the main ports on the planet and was always busy. They were one of many who were bartering for a storage bay to park their ship in for a week. Jay was grateful IA was footing the bill, as the prices were exorbitant. The relaxed air they'd developed on the ship was still present, but a fresh tension had formed as they stepped out of the bay. The mission had begun.

They each had a pack of supplies slung over their shoulder. They looked like any other travelers as they joined the crowd waiting for a transport shuttle to take them to the nearby city. Jay took a moment to look over the surroundings. The starport was built on top of a salt pan, with mountains encircling the large, flat surface. Miles of smooth salt merged into rock and dirt as it approached the harsh cliff face to the north. The city of Ashak rested on the top of the cliff. It had roads built into the rock that twisted up to the city center. Ashak had large buildings and bustling streets. It had started as a small trading settlement and had quickly grown. Its reputation and location remained unchanged, but its tendency toward illegal practices had risen, helped by the power and influence of the Kada'rah.

A tap on his arm drew Jay's attention. Tristan nodded to the left where the shuttle approached. When it landed and its passengers disembarked, a portion of the waiting crowd stepped inside. The shuttle was full of seats and poles to hold on to, and Tristan and Jay took a place standing together in the corner. The moment everyone was on board, the automated craft lifted into the air.

Tristan was looking out of the window, but Jay knew he was listening to the conversation between three nearby port workers. It held little interested to Jay — anger over budget cuts and AI support minimizing paid working hours — so he let his mind wander back to the city.

Jay had never visited Ashak, but IA had provided everything they could need — a map of the area, forecasted weather for the week and a dossier on animals and plants native to Asam and the Carana Desert. They had also included a list of dealers who would sell them sturdy equines. IA had information on the preferred breeds for their mission and current trading prices. It had been years since his time with the UCAFD, but they had never managed such thorough information. Jay supposed that was the difference between the soldiers and the spies.

Looking at Tristan, he wondered what had made the agent choose to be a spy. Had he been handpicked or had he naturally gravitated to the agency of secrets?

When the shuttle landed at the plaza, Jay let his eyes drift over the people darting from place to place. It was a large, open area with a balcony that overlooked the starport. People were chatting, eating and drinking.

There were even a few street performers. Jay suppressed a chuckle when he spotted at least three people being pickpocketed.

The buildings of the city spread up the mountainside in winding roads and narrow alleyways. There were bars and gambling dens galore. Ashak was the perfect place for a charlatan who needed to lie low but still craved some fun. It was a damn shame he and Tristan really weren't two thieves looking for a good drink and a comfortable bed. They could spend weeks here, living a life of debauchery and disrepute. They would have sex every night—and a few more times during the day. It sounded much more appealing than a rescue mission and going up against the Kada'rah.

Jay held on to the wistful idea for a few seconds longer, but the doors of the shuttle opened and it was time to focus.

Tristan exited the shuttle with a sly grin. He darted his eyes to the occasional pocket, as if he wanted to rob it. He was every inch the relaxed and ready vagabond. Jay was still surprised by how quickly Tristan could shift between one persona and another. It was a fascinating skill, but he didn't have the time to truly admire it.

Jay adjusted the pack on his shoulder and followed along at a lazy pace. A few real conmen glanced at them, but they were dismissed as difficult marks. The people of the city were not so willing to let them walk by unaccosted. The moment they left the plaza for the shaded city streets, the amount of people tripled.

Workers rushed from one side of the street to another, clearly in a hurry to get to their next destination. There were animals being led on ropes or dragging carts. Men and women shouted prices for their wares or bartered with shoppers who were desperate for a good deal. Large hovercraft zipped overhead while smaller road craft pushed through the churning streets, beeping their horns at the pedestrians in their way. It was a cacophony of sounds and languages. It made a person want to flee into the safety of an empty alleyway or the quieter plaza — right into the open, opportunistic arms of any good thief.

Within five minutes, two people had bumped against Jay, trying to steal from one of his pockets. He caught one by the wrist and glared until they'd retreated. The other he let graze his plasma gun before he caught their eye with a dark glower. Tristan sent similar, silent threats to approaching thieves and the attempts to steal from them soon halted.

Tristan and Jay didn't speak as they made their way through the mayhem, communicating only by eye contact and touches to the arm. Eventually the loud, bustling nature of the town center faded, and they reached the more slow-paced and better-quality stalls and shops. The stall they were looking for was easy to find. Rickety, wooden and old, most people would have walked right past it. It was run by a heavily tan old man with a pipe in his mouth. He sat comfortably on a high chair, his legs nowhere near the ground. The stall had pillows and a bed for quick naps. There were six datascreens with thin cracks on them. The area smelled of vanilla, cloves and tobacco. When they stopped in front of him, the man smiled around the pipe in his mouth but didn't say a word. They'd have to make the first move.

"We hear you're the one to see about a sturdy steed," Tristan said, offering a charming smile.

The man sucked on his pipe before expelling a thin smoke ring. He pulled the pipe from his lips and nodded.

"Fine quaggas, good price," the man said.

He gestured at a datascreen. Jay picked it up and turned it on, finding a record of the equines for sale and their prices. Tristan looked over Jay's shoulder. He tapped a picture of an equine, accessing further details on the quagga. They looked through twenty before choosing two stallions that met their requirements.

When they showed the man their choices, he nodded and took another puff from his pipe.

"Good boys." Jay couldn't tell if the compliment was for them or their selection. "Pay now and we will fetch them."

"How long will it take?" Tristan questioned.

The stall owner grinned before grabbing a different datascreen. He tapped it and glanced to his left. They had to take a step to the side to see, but Jay was surprised to find a transporter embedded in the road's stone. It was common in larger cities to have fresh wares transported from where they were housed and farmed, but Jay hadn't been expecting it on Asam. The IA had certainly picked someone with good quality. The price and use of a transporter spoke for itself.

"Excellent," Tristan said. "I'll transfer it."

The man set up the transaction before passing a datascreen to Tristan, who made the payment. Jay moved around Tristan to stand before the transporter. After being assured of the successful transfer of payment, the old man placed their order and the first quagga appeared in front of Jay.

The equine was tall and large, standing at his eye-level. It was a stallion, dark brown with black stripes around the head, neck and shoulders before his coat faded into a lighter brown. His legs were white, along with his tail, while his short mane had black and white stripes. The quagga already had a saddle and reins, and Jay took the reins and led the animal off the transporter. He smiled at the quagga's easy compliance and stroked the stallion's neck.

When his quagga was clear of the platform, Tristan took Jay's place and awaited their second purchase. This quagga was just as large but was a much lighter brown, with black stripes visible almost down to its rump. His mane and tail were the same as Jay's and he whinnied at seeing Jay's quagga, obviously familiar with the other stallion.

"Good ride to you," the old man said before placing the pipe back in his mouth and puffing away at it once more.

Jay gave him a nod of thanks. Tristan ignored him to lead his quagga away. Jay fell back into step beside the agent and waited until they were far enough away that no one would hear them before leaning close and asking, "Did you see the names on the quagga's dossiers?"

Tristan frowned. "Brutus and Rinax. What of it?"

"Nothing." Jay shrugged. "But you know what they say about naming animals." He stroked a hand down the quagga's neck for further emphasis. He looked at Tristan. "It makes them harder to give up."

Tristan looked unimpressed. "I doubt either of us are the sentimental type."

Jay looked at his quagga, Brutus. He was a docile and handsome animal, but it was true that he should just consider the equine as just one more piece of equipment. Rescuing Zanik then getting out alive was the priority. If it were him or the quagga, he wouldn't hesitate to make that choice. Yet Jay had always been fond of animals. He didn't want to leave them to the mercy of the Kada'rah or to wander the desert with a low chance of survival, if he could avoid it.

But life was tough, especially as a soldier's steed. These quaggas had just graduated into that unfortunate position.

Patting Brutus, Jay didn't respond to Tristan's remark as they stepped back into the bustle of the populated streets.

They still had a long way to go to reach the outskirts of Ashak.

The city was built into the cliff and had been forced to expand around the impenetrable rock. That caused it to have lots of steep, high streets only to plummet into low dips. When the buildings eventually stopped, the sophisticated roads turned into dirt trails that led to the wall of mountainous granite that surrounded the city.

At that point, trails shot off in all directions, taking explorers anywhere they wanted to go, including the Carana Desert, which spread for hundreds of miles on the other side of the mountain.

Caverns and caves needed to be navigated successfully if a person wanted to survive. One wrong turn could get someone lost, with little chance of rescue. It would take hours of mountain climbing to reach the desert and, once there, conditions would only get worse. Jay wasn't looking forward to it.

Welcome back to hell, Major.

The voice of his old drill sergeant passed through Jay's mind. The man had taken it as a personal challenge to break the spirit of every recruit under his command. Jay had taken it as a personal challenge to never give up. It meant that his drill sergeant's voice echoed in his head, reminding him to get up, get moving and walk off that broken leg he'd had.

'You'll rest when you're in bed, private.'

Jay let out a huff of breath and flicked his gaze to Tristan. The man was focused on the city and looking for a place to buy the last of their supplies. He was an antagonistic, clinical and perfectly poised agent who was the cause of Jay being a major again.

Yet despite all the annoyance and trouble, Jay still wanted to get a hand under Tristan's shirt and capture his lips in a kiss. But that was just his libido talking, and Jay would have to ignore it.

Because Tristan was right—neither of them did sentiment. It was why Brutus the quagga and Tristan the IA agent would end up meaning the same amount to Jay by the end of the week…absolutely nothing.

Right?

Chapter Five

Once, it had been common for people to cross the Carana Desert with quaggas. It had been a fast and easy way to reach the isolated settlements when few people had been able to access hovercrafts. However, as large swathes of the sand had become Kada'rah territory, people had been forced to take longer routes or pay to fly.

The villagers and occasional sightseer still journeyed across the sands, but it was dangerous if a person didn't know the areas to avoid. It meant that Jay and Tristan were a normal enough sight that no one raised any eyebrows. They'd planned to lie about where they were headed if anyone asked — but no one did. They bought a week's worth of supplies without a problem.

It was a winding walk to get free from the bustle of Ashak, but when they finally exchanged city streets for dirt tracks, the size of the rock wall bracketing the city could be truly absorbed. The towering mountainside could be seen from Ashak, but there were too many distractions in the city for it to hold anyone's attention.

Here though, the stone monolith even took away Jay's breath. The cliffs and crags loomed overhead. The jagged black rock stood higher than the tallest building, fallen boulders the size of a small hovercraft littered the sides of the track and stone spires jutted from the ground like teeth. The wall of stone flanked the city like a barricade, while the trail they needed disappeared from sight as it snaked through the treacherous terrain.

It would be hell, but Jay was thankful IA hadn't sent him to a jungle. Jay would take a hot, sand-coated environment over a humid, overgrown and bug-filled forest. The Carana Desert would be pleasant by comparison.

Stepping forward, Jay clicked his tongue to get Brutus trotting along behind him.

The trail was weathered from centuries of use and was easy to follow. Luckily there were no unstable patches. He led the quagga through the landscape without issue, feeling grateful that there were no snakes or other poisonous wildlife. The city sounds began to fade the farther they walked and the heavy footfalls of their quaggas echoed around the rock, but Jay and Tristan were silent.

Everything went peacefully until they reached the first cavern. The tunnel wasn't long and there was enough light filtering through the holes in the rock that it was well illuminated, but the enclosed space unnerved the quaggas. Jay gave Brutus a soft pat and stood in front of the equine. He murmured encouragement as he coaxed the quagga to follow him inside. The animal remained unhappy about entering the cave but he seemed to trust Jay's soothing voice and comforting strokes. They made it down the first slope and to a wider stretch of track without further problems. Jay stopped Brutus but continued to pat him as he waited for Tristan.

Unfortunately, the agent's quagga wasn't as cooperative.

Tristan was trying to guide the animal inside, but Rinax was refusing, shaking his head and stamping his feet. The agent was becoming increasingly frustrated. His voice was rising and becoming laced with irritation. That was only making the situation worse.

Moving to Brutus' side, Jay opened the small bag attached to the quagga's saddle and pulled out a corded pouch. After nudging it open with his fingers, Jay plucked out a sugar cube. Brutus was already turning to him with interest. Jay gave the treat to the quagga, who munched on it happily. Feeling confident that Brutus would stay inside the cavern, Jay patted the quagga one more time before making his way over to Tristan and Rinax.

"Here," Jay said when he reached them. He held out a sugar cube to the agent. "Tempt him with this and soften your voice."

Tristan didn't look pleased by Jay's involvement, but he did as he'd suggested.

Rinax remained unhappy, but the sugary sweet tempted him to follow Tristan inside. When they'd joined Brutus, Tristan let the quagga eat his reward. Jay slipped the satchel of cubes back into his pocket before taking Brutus' reins. The quagga's lips followed his hand, hoping to find more treats. Jay chuckled and showed him there was nothing there. Brutus huffed out a disappointed breath and Jay gave him a fond pat before leading him deeper inside.

The cavern was large, with the path big enough for them to stand side by side with the quaggas following behind. It was cooler as well, the beating sun unable to touch them through the dense rock. It was almost peaceful, but relaxing wasn't a luxury they had access to on a mission. He'd been briefed on anything that IA found relevant, though not Tristan's strengths and weaknesses. It was time to ask a few questions.

"Have you ever used quaggas before?"

There were a few seconds silence before Tristan admitted, "No."

Jay winced. He wished he'd known that before. They could have hired something else. It didn't bode well for their mission if Tristan wasn't a quick study. They needed to blend in and they wouldn't do that if Tristan couldn't lead a quagga – or if he fell out of his saddle at the first sign of trouble. Jay barely refrained from rubbing a weary hand over his face.

"Have you ridden other equines?" he asked.

Tristan glared. "I wouldn't have been recommended for this mission if I hadn't."

Jay frowned. That was unexpected but promising. "I thought you were here because you knew about the Kada'rah?"

"Yes," Tristan agreed. "But that would be useless if I couldn't handle field work." He turned a glare on his quagga. "My experience was with less-difficult mounts."

"The quagga isn't difficult," Jay said. "He's uncertain. You're new and this place is strange to him."

"Then he needs better training," Tristan muttered. When he spoke again, he raised his voice and insisted, "I can handle him, and I will *not* need help again."

He sounded indignant and Jay felt a flare of amusement, which he quickly hid. If Tristan saw his smile, it wouldn't go down well. Tristan was irritated enough without Jay provoking him—but it begged a question. Was Tristan defensive because he hadn't known how to tame the quagga or because he'd failed to do it front of Jay?

They were past the point of first impressions, but opinions and appearances still mattered, especially to an IA agent. Tristan had pride, and failing with the quagga had been a blow to it. Tristan probably wanted to prove himself not only as a field agent, but also as someone Jay could respect. He likely cared more than he let on about what Jay thought of him. Jay felt a need to ease Tristan's worry.

"Give him some time to get to know you," Jay said, his voice quiet and more weighted than he'd intended, "and he'll trust you more."

He wasn't just talking about the quaggas.

The agent caught his gaze, seemingly under-standing, and the moment stretched. Jay didn't know what Tristan was searching for in his expression, but whether or not he'd found it, he looked away.

"We don't have time for that," he said curtly. "And I don't need him to like me. I just need him to do his job."

Jay felt the sting of Tristan's words but refused to let it show. Cut and dried, clinical and meaningless, that was Tristan Fox. He was also dead wrong.

"A job like this needs trust," Jay answered, his voice sharpening. "He has to know you won't lead him astray, that he can follow your orders and not get killed for it."

"And can he trust me?" Tristan parried, holding Jay's gaze. "Can I trust *him*? Sometimes you don't have the luxury of confidence, Jay."

"Sometimes you just have to work harder to gain it," Jay argued back.

Tristan didn't reply immediately. His lips were thinned and his eyebrows furrowed in thought. This had never been about the quaggas and Jay was determined to keep going until he made his point. They had to make this mission work. Their relationship was built on lies and sexual tension, and they needed to change that. Ignoring the problem might be enough to get them to the Kada'rah compound, but would it still get them out alive? They had to work together — and that meant getting to know one another.

Jay was debating what else to say, how to move them forward, but Tristan beat him to it.

"My experiences have been with horses," Tristan said, surprising Jay. "It was never in terrain like this. I rode on immaculate properties or showgrounds with purebred mares."

Tristan held Jay's gaze. His expression was stubborn and brazen. It reminded Jay of Bryce, refusing to be outdone or lose a challenge. If Tristan was going to agree with Jay, then he'd dive in feet first.

"It was all about impressing and ensnaring my target," Tristan continued. "The horses knew their role as well as I did, and my missions rarely took me out of a city." He raised his eyebrows. "I suppose yours rarely took you near civilization."

Tristan was prompting him. The agent had opened up and now he expected Jay to do the same. It was an arrogant presumption, yet somehow Jay liked it.

"The extractions I worked didn't take place in populated cities," Jay acknowledged. "They call different people in for those. I've often used quaggas on missions, as the UCAFD trains them. They're good in the desert, and they're loyal."

Tristan nodded and some of the tension in the air dissipated.

"Where I was, you'd never see a quagga," Tristan remarked. "I'll work him out soon enough."

Jay started to nod but stopped as he made the connection. He couldn't keep silent.

"They had you at the Athena Racecourse."

Athena only had the purest and more prized equines. There were dozens of events for a stallion or mare to participate in — racing, jumping, beauty contests — the list went on. Unfortunately, quaggas had a reputation for being used by the working class. They might be a handsome animal with good breeding, but the society that flocked to Athena wouldn't want to see something so common.

Athena was a place for the rich to indulge themselves and try to upstage one another. Everyone knew everyone and a third of the people who attended had a criminal empire. Being able to slip in and out undetected was a testament to Tristan's skill.

"That's impressive," Jay said. "You'd have to be damn good to blend in there."

Tristan's lips curved into a proud smile. The agent didn't confirm his presence there, but Jay could tell he was right.

It was no wonder Tristan had fooled Jay so easily. A small-time thief was a walk in the park compared to an elitist racing society gentleman. Tristan was a damn good spy. He was a deceiving, conniving, perfect example of IA training. So, if Jay hated spies so much, why did he still find Tristan incredibly attractive?

Jay had always appreciated someone who was competent, but this was something else. Every word out of Tristan's mouth intrigued Jay further. He wanted to unravel the mystery and learn how Tristan ticked. He wouldn't mind unwrapping Tristan again too, if he were being honest.

It was a real problem.

They would be alone together for days, and Jay needed to keep a level head. They would end up talking and getting to know each other on the mission—that was important—but he couldn't let anything else happen. He sure as hell couldn't get attached or infatuated. Strengths and weaknesses... That was what he needed to focus on. Mission statistics.

"What kind of riding did you do there?" Jay inquired.

"Mounted archery and jumps were my specialty."

The images that were brought to mind weren't helping Jay's conviction. Tristan sitting atop his mare with windswept hair and a bow in hand... He'd have been a few years younger and wearing bright-colored riding clothes. Tristan's control of the mare would be perfect, and his eyes would be alert and intense.

It was a shame Jay had never seen it.

Those strong thighs would be in tight-fitting cotton and Tristan's pale cheeks would be flushed with the thrill of victory. How many awards had he won—or had IA specified he couldn't overperform? They wouldn't want their agent making galactic news, his face broadcasted for all to see. No, Tristan would be out of the running early. He'd be able to get into all the important places, but no one would look at him unless they wanted to offer sympathy.

Jay wouldn't have offered condolences to the losing rider. He'd have pressed the agent against the nearest hard surface and teased him for losing when he should have won the trophy. Tristan would forget about his mission to argue, just to get his mouth on Jay's. They'd go somewhere private and remind themselves that Tristan was a hot-blooded man underneath Agent Fox's professional demeanor.

It was a really nice fantasy. Jay could have toyed around with it for hours, but it was just that — a fantasy, and an impossible one at that. They weren't on Athena, and even if they were, Tristan had made it clear that a single night for defusing their sexual tension was all they would share. The agent wouldn't allow a quickie beneath the sand dunes or some groping against the cavern wall. It was all about the mission and Jay needed to follow suit.

Zanik Taziv...the reason he was here. The Qui's life hung in the balance, and Jay wouldn't let lust distract him from saving Zanik or gaining his clean slate.

"We shouldn't need you to do jumps or archery here," Jay said, "which is a good thing, since quaggas are crap at it." He kept his eyes averted and changed the subject. "You got the map handy?"

"You don't care about the map," Tristan said, his eyes burning into Jay. "Your mind wandered and now you're on edge. What were you thinking about?"

Jay's mind immediately jumped back to the two of them against a wall, with Tristan in a riding uniform. He refused to be flustered.

"Does it matter?"

"Yes," Tristan answered. "You said we need trust, but we also need to understand each other's moods and work together under pressure. What unsettled you? If it's going to reoccur, we need to deal with it now."

Tristan's blunt words made Jay want to respond in kind, to push back and throw the agent off guard. Jay caught and held Tristan's gaze.

"I wasn't unsettled," he replied. "I was imagining being on Athena, stripping you of your riding clothes and having you against a wall."

Tristan swallowed and desire flared to life in his eyes. Jay's pulse spiked. He wasn't the only one who found that idea attractive.

"I see," Tristan murmured, his voice lowering. He darted his tongue out to wet his lips, capturing Jay's attention. "We were meant to have dealt with that."

Jay held Tristan's darkened gaze. "And have you dealt with it?"

Tristan's eyes dropped to Jay's mouth then away, where he focused on the rocks. His reactions answered the question.

"We can't afford distractions," he stated firmly.

Jay was tempted to disagree, to point out how long and lonely desert nights could be when far from home. It would be a few days until they were in enemy territory. There was plenty of time to work off some of their desire.

But where Jaybird might have a policy of laughing in the face of danger and where Heath Chapman might still crack a joke in the middle of Armageddon, there were limits. Sex in the middle of a mission risked getting them killed.

"Okay," Jay said. "We're attracted to each other, but we don't act on it."

"Precisely."

Tristan's voice was smooth once more and his face had cleared of any remaining desire, like an actor changing roles. Tristan was prim and professional once more. He started leading the quagga without another glance at Jay. Jay could almost hear the walls being erected between them. He could have let it lie, but that wasn't smart. They both knew the importance of working together. Burying their attraction might be the only option, but that didn't mean they should stop talking. Soldiers had a brotherhood, and they needed to forge something similar. Jay racked his brain for a new subject to discuss as he caught up to Tristan.

When he alighted on a memory from a few years before, he chuckled. It was a story he often told but had never got around to sharing with Bryce. It would break the tension and might even earn him one of Tristan's elusive smiles.

"You know, I once spent a pleasant night sharing a stable with some quagga and burro foals."

Jay patted Brutus' neck, remembering the curious and affectionate nature of the foals when he'd cuddled up against them. Tristan looked at him, unable to fight the draw of curiosity.

"Why were you sleeping in a stable?"

"I started a bar fight after someone challenged me to a game of darts." Jay smirked. "I won, and they weren't happy with me."

Tristan rolled his eyes but he looked amused. His body was angled toward Jay, his expression filled with interest, so Jay continued. "I avoided most of the thrown furniture and walked away with a good bottle from behind the counter."

"Which you drank, causing you to stumble into the nearest building at some ungodly hour," Tristan guessed dryly.

Jay did a double-take. Had he told Tristan the story before or was he that predictable? Either way, Tristan was waiting expectantly with a smile tugging at his lips. Who was Jay to disappoint him?

"It was a nice way to spend the night, until the stable hand found me the next morning and started shouting."

Tristan snorted and shook his head. Normally, Jay would continue with his usual flourish and mention how his charm and good looks had given him a true 'roll in the hay', but at the last moment, Jay stopped. The real truth about his stories were that most of them were overdramatized to captivate his audience. He would use them to convince someone into his bed or win himself another drink at the bar. Tristan might not be a fellow soldier in the classic sense, but there was something to be said about honor. Tall tales were one thing, but if he wanted to trust Tristan and have the spy be honest with him, Jay had to return the favor.

"I didn't actually," Jay answered. Tristan looked confused. "Drain the bottle," he elaborated. "I hardly touched it." A rueful smile formed. "It's plain stupid to drink when you can't trust the people around you. I slept in the stables because it was cold that night and the man I'd beaten was staying in the same inn." Jay shrugged. "I traded the stolen bottle for the stablehand's silence and made my way back to my ship."

Tristan narrowed his eyes. "I doubt that's a version of events you often tell people."

"No," he agreed, "but you're right. We need to work well together. A good place to begin is with honesty."

"That is a good start," Tristan acknowledged, "but it isn't something I expected you'd offer willingly."

Jay felt offended. "Did you think everything I said before was a lie? Or something I wouldn't stick to?"

"I expected what I get from any UCAFD soldiers forced to work with IA agents," Tristan stated. "You close ranks when you're together and you give nothing more than the bare minimum when you're apart. You distrust us on principle and cooperate as a last and desperate resort."

Jay winced and looked away. IA didn't have a good reputation among soldiers and were the butt of many jokes. Jay knew that IA served a purpose and was doing an important job, just like any extraction team, but they often conflicted with each other. IA also reported on a soldier's conduct if they came across the UCAFD during a mission. It left a bad taste in many mouths. Yet despite their willingness to spy on soldiers, at the end of the day they shared the same goal as the UCAFD — to protect the universe.

Jay could also understand better than most why pointing out bad behavior and misconduct was necessary. Sometimes, a spy was exactly what someone needed — that, or a presumed-dead witness.

"We spoke about equines, Jay," Tristan continued, pulling Jay from his memories, "and other facts of no consequence. How was I to know you'd continue where it mattered?"

Jay stopped walking and Tristan did the same. There was a different tension between them now, the kind Jay had experienced in training rooms when he was sizing up a new member of the team. Tristan was eyeing him carefully and Jay knew this was a battle they needed to put behind them if they wanted to move forward.

"You know I'm not a soldier anymore," Jay began.

Tristan laughed, cutting off further words.

"No," he admitted, "you're a thief who spent months spinning ridiculous tales to a starry-eyed waiter who didn't know any better. But I'm not him. I'm an IA agent. The major would hate me on instinct and the thief would want to avoid me. So, where does that leave us, Jaybird? Because I can't figure it out."

Tristan's words were laced with frustration, the same kind that had appeared when he'd struggled with Rinax. He was clearly floundering and he hated it. They were still leaning in and pulling away like they had in the diner, but it was no longer smooth or enjoyable. They were trying to find their footing in a strange new terrain, and more than just their lives depended on it.

"It leaves us in the middle of nowhere, Tristan," he said. "It means we have to make this work because there's no other option." He smiled ruefully. "That's the thing about soldiers and spies. Spies know that everyone is lying about something, and they try to figure out what it is. Soldiers know that everyone is just trying to survive. Soldiers don't have the time to do anything but hold blind faith that the man beside them is on their side."

Tristan raised his eyebrows. "Are you suggesting I adopt blind faith?"

"I'm saying it would make things easier, but it's probably contrary to your nature and your training." Jay softened his words with a grin. "So how about we settle for telling the truth when we can and avoiding a lie when we can't?"

Tristan's face remained blank, but Jay wasn't bothered by it. They'd made great leaps and bounds in their partnership already. They'd aired their concerns and managed to be honest about it. The rest would come with time. It was better to let Tristan chew on everything and come to an opinion.

Clicking his tongue, Jay encouraged Brutus to start walking again. But he didn't get far before Tristan spoke.

"They asked me for an assessment on your character."

Jay stopped and looked back at the other man. Tristan remained motionless, his face showing nothing.

"They asked if we could trust you on the mission and if I was comfortable working with you," Tristan explained. "Your skills and history during the UCAFD were perfect, but your time away had the agency worried. No one could be sure if you were a practical risk."

"But you endorsed me." Jay realized that fact with some awe.

"Yes," Tristan admitted, "I did."

A smile pulled at Tristan's mouth and his eyes were flooding with amusement.

"Soldiers might have blind faith but *spies*" — and the way he used Jay's description was cheerfully mocking — "make more educated deductions."

Jay laughed, surprise and pleasure bursting through him. Jay didn't know why it mattered, but he felt satisfied knowing that Tristan had advocated for him. Tristan, for all their history and his standoffish nature, had chosen to work with him. Jay knew they would still argue, but this was a more positive start than Jay had expected. In fact, it pleased him more than it probably should.

"Well," Jay remarked, "maybe there's hope for us after all."

Tristan's smile widened before he coaxed his quagga forward. Rinax followed the agent without hesitation this time, and they set off once more. The silence returned, but this time it was more comfortable. The air had been cleared and the ground rules settled. They would likely continue to poke and prod at each other as the journey went on, but for the moment, Jay was content.

They understood how to proceed, and for less than a day's work, it was a good start.

* * * *

When they exited the other side of the cavern, the track split in three directions. They took the one on the left and were soon walking on a narrow path that forced them to move in single file. The trail was full of steep inclines and there were places where the ground was more rubble than road. There was a perilous and winding section carved into the rock with a ravine on one side. Despite knowing people walked it frequently, Jay still expected it to collapse beneath them.

It was a slow process that took them four hours, but finally, they neared the end of the mountain range. The dirt underneath their feet started to turn from dark brown to light yellow. Rocks and struggling desert plants spattered the landscape. The wind was carrying grains of sand that caught against their skin while the oppressive desert heat was making itself known.

They remained protected from the sun by the shadows of the rock face, but when they came around the last corner, Jay slowed to a stop. He stared out at miles of sand, disrupted only by dry shrubs and stunted trees. When they walked farther into the Carana Desert, fewer plants and animals would be found until nothing but dunes remained. There were a few oases across the desert, but the Kada'rah would guard them viciously. It would be a hot, demanding and challenging journey, with little chance of relief. Jay was already longing for a shower.

Sighing, Jay grabbed the material bunched around his neck, pulling it over his head to form the hood that would protect him from the sun. Tristan did the same beside him, even pulling the shemagh up over the lower half of his face.

When Jay stepped out onto the sand with his quagga following behind him, he could almost believe he'd never left the UCAFD. His uniform would have been heavy and familiar on his back and a plasma gun would never have been far from his reach. He could almost hear the footfalls of a group of soldiers behind him and the boisterous chatter of his unit — but it went as quick as it had come and Jay blinked away the memories.

Shaking it off, he moved his attention to Brutus, giving the quagga's gear a quick inspection before climbing into the saddle. It had been a while since he'd ridden, but it wasn't a skill a person forgot. Tristan mounted his own equine and the two of them exchanged a brief glance before they started off.

The information IA had given them said they would need to head north for thirty miles before curving to the northeast for another fifty until they reached the

Kada'rah stronghold. Their first day and night on the sands would be easy. They would travel in territory still frequented by travelers and tourists. The syndicate wouldn't patrol it and they'd be left alone. The second day would have them in Kada'rah territory, where they would need to be careful about being seen. It wouldn't be until the third day that they would reach the closely monitored areas surrounding the compound. They would have to proceed on foot, staying out of sight and slipping into the building unseen.

The plan was to perform a silent, perfect extraction. Jay doubted it would work. This wasn't the kind of place filled with blind spots and dim-witted guards. Tristan would need a distraction to get anywhere near Zanik. Jay would have to cause chaos and explosions if this was going to succeed. He still wasn't happy to perform an extraction without a team. He would feel more confident if he had additional men at his back, but he didn't have a choice. His priority was getting Zanik to safety — by whatever means necessary.

Focusing his attention on the steady steps of Brutus, Jay forced aside his worry. The quagga's repetitive movements lulled him into a state of calm as they crossed onto the sand. Jay was never unaware of the landscape and what might lurk over a dune, but he let himself unwind.

A few hovercraft flew overhead and there was even a caravan of travelers in the distance, but there was little else to break the monotony. Nothing but Tristan… The agent was beside him, his hands loosely holding the reins and his blue eyes examining the distant caravan.

"Too bad there weren't more people to spare," Jay remarked, "or we might have been traveling in style."

He gestured at the caravan, prompting Tristan to shake his head.

"And become a giant beacon? I would rather be alone with a quagga."

"But you're not alone," Jay responded. "You have me."

He followed the flirtation with an instinctive wink. It was only in the silence that followed that he realized what he'd done.

"It's a habit for you to do that, isn't it?" Tristan asked.

Jay didn't bother to deny it. "Charm has saved my life on more than one occasion."

"You call that charm, do you?"

Jay took a moment before he caught the humor in Tristan's eyes. When he realized the man was teasing him, Jay smiled.

"I...and many others," Jay agreed.

"Clearly you all have bad taste."

Jay chuckled, and a comment about how susceptible Tristan had been at the diner was on his tongue, but he held it in at the last moment. Tristan had been on a mission. His thoughts and feelings on Jay's flirtations were unclear. It was better to avoid joking about it.

So, he tried a different tactic.

"Then what would Tristan Fox consider an example of good charm?"

"Something that makes a person blush rather than roll their eyes."

"Neither of us are the type to blush," Jay pointed out.

"Then maybe we're not the right people to charm?" Tristan suggested. His eyes caught Jay's. "Perhaps we prefer blunt honesty."

Jay's lips twitched, but he quelled his smile. "Is that your way of asking to know about my thoughts on Athena?"

Tristan laughed, the sound sudden and sharp. He'd startled it out of the agent and Jay felt proud of his success. Tristan had gotten himself under control, but his grin still lingered.

"No, that wasn't my intention."

"Then we'd better find something else to talk about." Jay soon alighted on an idea. "You said my charm is bad, but I can't be the worst you've heard. Bryce must have gained his share of terrible one-liners."

"He did," Tristan agreed neutrally.

"Then let's hear them. We've got a long ride ahead of us." Jay gestured at the unending sands. "Give me something to laugh about."

Tristan looked thoughtful before he declared, "Do you need someone to wash that apron? I'd gladly pick up your clothes tomorrow morning."

Jay blinked. "You're kidding."

"No," Tristan said dryly, "I'm not."

Jay whistled. "A laundry pickup line. I expected better from the workmen of Vicente."

"Oh, I have worse."

Jay shifted in his saddle and walked Brutus a little closer. He looked at Tristan with anticipation and settled in for a good laugh. Tristan rolled his eyes, but even with the shemagh covering his lips, Jay knew the agent was smiling.

They spoke about bad flirtations for the first hour, which soon changed to people they had dealt with, both in and out of the job. Jay had numerous stories about foolish men and women he'd met in bars or in the criminal world. Tristan had an unending supply of people who'd taken his pretty face to mean he didn't have a brain between his ears.

They didn't speak for the entire journey. Sometimes the heat became too oppressive or their throats felt dry from the sun and sand. But whenever they stopped, it took no effort at all to start back up again.

They stopped twice to rest and hydrate the quaggas, using the break to check their direction and discuss the minute changes to their route. When Jay stood close to Tristan, all he could smell was leather, sweat and a hint of a woodsy fragrance. He could also tell how the temperature and harshness of the desert was hitting Tristan harder than him. The agent was bringing a hand to rub his neck, tension from the ride resting in his shoulders. A wet cloth dabbed over his face wasn't enough to remove the flush from his pale skin. The desert was hardest the first time a person dealt with it. The constant, exhausting heat, the endless expanse of sand and the complete detachment from anything resembling civilization... It was like getting a glimpse of eternity.

"Come on," Jay murmured, squeezing Tristan's shoulder in commiseration. "A few more hours and we can set up camp." He grinned. "Night always makes the desert worth it."

Tristan didn't look like he believed Jay's words, but he still climbed back onto Rinax and prepared to start the next leg of the trek. Jay did the same, patting Brutus' neck before directing him forward. This time, he started the first story, hoping to gain Tristan's smile.

The next section of desert was much the same as the first. They had small breaks every few hours to stretch their legs and refresh, but Jay could see Tristan's good humor and energy fading. It was a blessing when the sun started to drop toward the horizon, bringing with it the promise of cool night air. Asam's temperature didn't drop as much as some planets Jay had been on, but he would greatly welcome any respite.

They'd done well for their first day. Asam had a twenty-seven-hour day, and they'd spent a good portion of it on the sand. When they finally brought their quaggas to a stop, it was late afternoon and Jay already felt better without the sun on his back. Tristan pulled off his hood with relief, running his fingers through his sweat-dampened hair and tilting his face into the breeze. Jay smiled, happy to let the agent take a few minutes to rest.

Pulling down his hood, Jay turned his attention to the quaggas. He gave them water and spread out some feed before unloading the supplies and equipment that he and Tristan would need for the night. The quaggas munched happily, allowing Jay to pull out the hobbles. The items were made of leather and there were two for each equine. They attached to the quagga's front and back legs, with a rope in the middle. There was one hobble for each side of the animal and it kept them from wandering during the night. When Jay bent down to strap them, he heard the rustling sound of Tristan opening the other supplies. When Jay finished, he gave a firm stroke to the forehead and neck of each equine. He also slipped them each a sugar cube as a reward for their good work.

Turning back to the makeshift camp, Jay found Tristan had already unrolled their bedding. It was designed for someone who wanted to travel light. Simple and compact, there was a bedroll for each of them that they could lie on or unzip, which could then be wrapped around their body for extra warmth. The top of the roll had a collapsible miniature tent for resting one's head inside to protect from wind and, in their case, sand.

Tristan was looking down at the bedding with discomfort. It was only for a moment, but he looked depressed as his hand came to knead his sore neck again. When Tristan noticed Jay watching, he dropped his hand and hid his discomfort.

"Asam's nightly temperatures shouldn't drop low enough to need a fire," Tristan said.

He was already moving to unpack the other items Jay had unloaded. Once again, the man refused to show any hint of weakness.

"No," Jay replied, "but we should use one while we have the chance. You can't do much to improve a soldier's rations, but cooking them does help."

If possible, Tristan looked even more drained. Jay wanted to wrap a sympathetic arm around the man's shoulders. Tristan's last mission might have meant working long hours in a diner, but he could go home to a proper bed and eat what he wished. This wasn't what he was used to.

"Be happy we don't have to hunt," Jay offered, trying to cheer him up. "You don't always luck out on that front."

"A lack of food to find?" Tristan asked

Jay grimaced, partly for show and partly in memory. "Or things that taste worse than your rations."

He was rewarded by seeing Tristan's curiosity and amusement return. "Oh?"

"I suppose my platoon should have realized that if there was a high population of lizards that nothing was eating, there was probably a reason. But our information said they were edible, so we figured we'd give them a shot." Jay shook his head. "Big mistake."

The squad had learned the hard way why no one, not even the predators, touched them, but they'd been running out of supplies and there had been nothing else to eat. It had become a game in the end, with one person eating their lizard while the rest of the platoon cheered them on. It had been a small burst of good humor amid a giant mess of a mission. No one had died and the mission had been a success, but they'd been stranded an extra week in the desert waiting for the UCAFD to extract them.

Recounting the story, however, was an easy way to fill the time, as he and Tristan prepared a place to light their fire and cook their meal. Throughout the recounting, Tristan would chuckle at him, an indulgent smile on his lips as he prompted Jay at all the right moments. Tristan seemed to forget about the pain in his neck and shoulders as Jay wove a tale that was humorous and slightly exaggerated but entirely true.

It was one of the first times in years that Jay had told a story from his days in the UCAFD. He forgot sometimes just how much he'd loved it, how much he missed his friends.

Sleep well, boys, Jay thought, staring at the fire as it crackled to life, a sad smile on his lips. *You deserve your peace.*

Chapter Six

"I didn't think it would look like this."

Jay glanced over at Tristan. The agent's palms were braced in the sand as he stared up at the sky with wondering eyes. Jay smiled and tilted his head back to admire the view too. The night sky was beautiful. The four moons of Asam were visible and bright. Two were full and their light cast a violet hue over the sand. The stars spread out across the rest of the sky, making it look endless and as if there was no horizon. The occasional shooting star could be spotted, and this far into the Carana Desert, there was almost no visible air traffic. A sky would never be so clear in the center of a city, and while Jay had seen several desert skies in his time, Asam offered one of the best.

His gaze lingered on Vicente. Jay could see the light of settlements, and somewhere among them would be the once-smoldering diner. Things had been simple before the Kada'rah had attacked. His gaze tracked to Bizantha, the other, larger moon. It was close enough to pick out the spaceport. Jay had been there prior to

Vicente—living it up, pretending to get drunk and taking meaningless flings back to his hotel room. He'd come to Vicente for a change of pace.

He'd never visited the other two moons. They were farther away and not as full, but they only added to the beautiful backdrop of space. It was a breathtaking sight. No wonder Tristan was admiring it.

Jay looked back at the man to find he hadn't moved. His expression was awed and peaceful. He looked younger and not as harsh. It could have been Jay and Bryce, off on a whirlwind trip to Asam for some sex in the sand. Yet, for all that it would be easier with the hapless waiter, Jay liked his time with the capable Tristan Fox more. It was dangerous, but Jay still wanted to know more about him.

"What did you think it would look like?" Jay asked.

"Like a normal sky." He chuckled. "I don't think I've looked up at the stars since my academy days."

"Dreaming of where your assignments would take you," Jay agreed, remembering the feeling all too well. "Picturing the universe at your feet."

Tristan flashed him a brief look of understanding before his gaze was back on the stars.

"It reminds me of a meteor shower," Tristan remarked. "It was my second year at Bayview and—"

"You were at Bayview?" Jay interrupted with surprise. "What years?"

Bayview was one of the top four military academies in the galaxy and where Jay had trained. It was one of the newer facilities, with high circular towers. They were filled with winding staircases and classrooms that overlooked the grounds. The academy was on a large property with lakes, grassy clearings and forests. It was picturesque, if not for the ever-changing obstacle courses, traps and non-active soldiers camping on the grounds waiting to capture unsuspecting students. The school's unorthodox methods had helped it to train some of the best stealth operatives in recent decades.

Bayview had a simple system. If someone wanted to visit the nearby city when they didn't have classes, they were welcome to — but there was a catch. They couldn't take the front door. They dared everyone to prove that they had what it took to be a soldier. They wanted anyone who wished to leave to make their way through the grounds without being caught. Jay had spent some of his best nights at the academy flushed with the success of evading or capturing the soldiers who were keeping him and his friends from leaving the academy.

It had all been in good fun, and making his way through undetected or imprisoning opponents gained a person higher marks in class. It could even help someone get specialized placement when their training was finished. It was how Jay had ended up in extraction.

"I was there from eighty-six to eighty-nine," Tristan answered, bringing Jay back from his thoughts. "Your records stated you were there from eight-five to eighty-eight."

It didn't surprise Jay that Tristan had memorized his military file. It made him wonder if Tristan had brought up Bayview deliberately. But did it matter? What ulterior motive could Tristan have for talking about their training days?

"Yeah," Jay confirmed. "And I remember the meteor shower from eighty-seven. I watched it from the grounds with my classmates. It was impressive."

Tristan's expression was smug. "I watched it from the roof."

Jay jerked his head to the other man. "The roof? That's impossible! There were more than a dozen locks and passcodes to get onto the roof!"

"And much like the grounds, you could get in and out of anywhere if you tried hard enough." Tristan grinned. "And making my way in and out of places without detection made IA interested in me."

Jay narrowed his eyes. "You couldn't have been undetected if they knew about it."

"You're right," he laughed. "The instructors were always watching to see who succeeded, who failed and who continued to try again, regardless."

"And they spotted you."

He'd seen it firsthand. After his third successful run through the forest, his instructors had met with him after class. They'd offered him alternative courses to what he'd already chosen. They were invitation only and for the specialized training they believed Jay would excel in—and they had been right.

"Yes, they spotted me," Tristan agreed. He was watching Jay carefully. "And they spotted you too. A man brilliant at making his way through enemy lines undetected to achieve his goal was a true extraction specialist."

Tristan's gaze held respect and admiration. Jay knew Tristan could be pretending, playing him for some secret mission, but Jay couldn't keep thinking like that. They had to trust each other. Second guessing, doubts and distrust would get them killed. Jay couldn't trust the UCAFD again and he had his doubts about IA, but out in the field, he could let himself trust Tristan.

"And you must have been just as good yourself," Jay replied. "Catching IA's attention and getting your way onto the roof was no small feat." Jay remembered his own attempts with amusement. "I once planned to scale the building with my friends, but we could never figure out a way to get past the locks without breaking them."

"You needed an infiltration specialist," Tristan advised with a grin.

Jay laughed and winked at the other man. "It seems I needed you."

Tristan's eyes danced at the tease. Jay expected him to make another mocking comment about Jay's attempts at flirtation, but he side-stepped it entirely.

"I doubt I would have interested you back then," Tristan said. "I was very self-assured."

"And you aren't now?"

Tristan didn't deign to acknowledge that with a comment, saying instead, "I was also fast-tracked and two years younger than those in my year."

Jay winced. Tristan was whipcord thin, toned and tall, but all of that came with growth spurts and training. He would have been just out of his teens when he had been at Bayview, scrawny and knobbly-kneed until he'd filled out. In comparison, Jay had spent his youth playing sports or flying his hoverboard into places where he wasn't supposed to be. He'd had muscles and strength long before his training had kicked in. Jay had been popular with friends all over Bayview, both in years above and below him. He didn't think Tristan had been as lucky.

Maybe that's why it's so easy for him to lose himself in a role and work alone, Jay thought, saddened to realize that the brotherhood of a platoon might be something Tristan had never experienced.

"Bayview had to have been tough," Jay said quietly. "Did you have many friends? People you trained with?"

Tristan laughed. "I might have been a brat, Jay, but I still had friends." Jay grinned, pleasantly surprised to have his assumption turned on its head. "But training for IA meant that my pool of friends was composed of people pre-selected by the agency."

"Soldiers and spies," Jay summarized.

It was a divide Jay hadn't noticed back in his academy days. He'd assumed it was the typical friendship groups forming rather than everyone either subconsciously of deliberately sectioning themselves into different organizations.

"Like-minds," Tristan corrected. His attention was locked on Jay. "But we can still find them in the oddest places."

"I think you're flattering me again, Tristan," Jay teased, a pleasant rush of warmth going through him at the look in the other man's eyes. "Has the desert heat been getting to you?"

Shaking his head with amused exasperation, Tristan turned his gaze back to the sky.

"I liked our conversations at the diner, Jay. I liked them today too. We proposed honesty and trust." He turned to Jay. "I can honestly say I'm enjoying the novelty of working with someone I consider capable."

That surprised Jay, but the warmth in his chest grew and spread.

I liked our conversations too, Jay thought, *but I like these more.*

The words should have been easy to say, but they felt slippery on his tongue. He cleared his throat but they still wouldn't come out, so Jay changed tracks to something easier but no less true.

"It's been a while since I've worked with someone capable too," Jay admitted. "Not a lot can be said for the company of thieves." Jay's eyes drifted to the fire, seeing a dozen faces he'd never forget. "And it's been a long time since I've had a mission."

The quiet lingered before Tristan asked, "Why did you leave the UCAFD?"

Jay jerked from his thoughts, his shoulders tensing. *Friendly talks. Ulterior motives. Information gathering.* It all became perfectly clear.

His voice was bitter as he said, "I thought that would be in my file."

Tristan stiffened from his relaxed sprawl. The lightness and good humor of their conversation disappeared in the blink of an eye.

"They redacted your records," Tristan explained, his voice cautious, as if he were wary of a fight. "It wasn't information they gave me, so I thought I would ask you."

Of course they redacted it, Jay thought spitefully. *They wanted to pretend it never happened.*

Fury rushed through Jay, but he knew the emotion wasn't helpful. It would cloud his mind and keep him from thinking clearly. He gritted his teeth and took calm breaths, trying to push his emotions aside and be impartial.

What had happened would cause untold damage to the Universal Collective if the public learned about it. He'd gained an honorable discharge, kept all his medals and gained compensation. His contract had been terminated with no complications. Major Heath Chapman remained a war hero and no one outside the need-to-know had learned the full story. There had been hundreds of missions running at the same time as Jay's. Soldier's names were rarely revealed in reports so that the men and women could be protected. There was no way for Tristan to know that Jay had been part of what had amounted to a massacre, where he'd been one of the few left alive to bring the traitors to justice. There was no reason for IA to entrust Tristan with such information—just like there was no reason for Jay to explain.

He wouldn't pick apart old wounds just to sate an agent's curiosity. Tristan's career might involve working out what he wasn't meant to know, but Jay wouldn't hand it out on a silver platter, not even for the sake of building trust.

"If IA didn't give you clearance, then you don't need to know," Jay said, his voice hard and unyielding.

Tristan's eyes narrowed, studying Jay, but if he tried to push it, he wouldn't get anywhere. Tristan might be like a dog with a bone, but Jay wouldn't break easily.

"I asked about it to get to know you, not for the sake of the mission," Tristan said, "but I won't press you."

Jay still felt agitated and on edge. Tristan backing down surprised him, but Jay's ease with the conversation had evaporated. How long would it be until he was asked again?

"So was that your side mission while we're here?" Jay asked. "To work out why I left? Why I became who I am?"

He'd been questioned a hundred times over why he'd left. Soldiers he'd trained with had recognized him and wanted to know what had happened. He never explained, no matter what they'd said or offered. Once he'd thrown himself into becoming Jaybird, the questions stopped. They were either disgusted to find out that he'd become a thief and wanted nothing to do with him or they stopped recognizing him.

"As I've said," Tristan said softly, clearly trying to remain unthreatening, "it's more of a personal interest than an assignment."

Jay couldn't trust it. He turned his back to Tristan, focusing on the desert surrounding them. It was calm and peaceful, with not another soul for miles. The quaggas were sleeping after a long day and the crackling of the fire and faint sounds of nocturnal wildlife were all he could hear. Jay looked at Vicente once more, letting the beauty of the sky and surrounding landscape soften the hackles that Tristan had raised.

It took him a few minutes before he was finally willing to speak. "I don't like to talk about why I left, Tristan."

"Yeah, I noticed that," Tristan drawled.

Jay's lips twitched, and he looked over his shoulder at the man. The light from the moon shadowed Tristan's skin, but his wry smirk was still visible.

"If you want to work me out," Jay advised him, "do it a different way."

"Noted," Tristan answered — and just like that, they both relaxed.

The silence returned, but Jay shifted so that his back wasn't to the agent. He poked at the fire and Tristan turned back to the stars. When Jay spoke again, it was almost by accident.

"I've missed this," Jay murmured, the words slipping free. "Camping on different worlds and looking up at an unfamiliar sky…" He ran his stick through the sand, creating patterns with no meaning. "I've missed relying on myself, rather than my ship."

There was a beat where nothing happened.

"I've missed being around someone who knows who I am," Tristan replied. "I've missed being able to work with someone and not only rely on them, but like them."

Jay smiled at the mutual understanding.

"It helps that we liked each other before either of us knew who the other was."

"Yes," Tristan agreed. "It's a pity we'll only have one mission together." Jay finally turned to him. Tristan's eyes stayed fixed on the stars. "I think we complement each other well."

We do. It's only been a few hours and I know that already.

Jay didn't want to think about how well they slotted together. They lived in different worlds and neither of them would give up the lives they'd created. This was a brief crossover and a desperate partnership, nothing more.

I'll be leaving the moment we've got Zanik back, Jay reminded himself. *Don't get attached.*

"Maybe we do," Jay answered. "Too bad our real lives get in the way."

Tristan sounded disappointed when he acknowledged, "Jaybird the thief."

"Agent Fox," Jay answered.

Two worlds that were too different to ever align for long... Tristan would never drop his career in IA to slum around as a thief, and Jay wasn't about to throw himself into the rules and regulations of an agency that wouldn't want him anyway.

He liked Tristan—and that was a hard pill to swallow. He hadn't liked anyone in years—but that wasn't enough. Jay wanted to kiss and undress him and press in close, but desire didn't cut it either. Real life sure as hell wasn't a fairy tale and Jay had to be prepared to walk away when their assignment was finished. It was the way it had to be.

"We should rest," Jay announced into the silence. "We've got an early morning."

He could feel Tristan's gaze on him like a physical weight, but eventually he heard the man shift. Jay glanced over to find Tristan dusting down his clothes and moving to his bedroll. Jay used some sand to douse the fire and keep it from smoking before using the light of the moons to make his way to his own bed. Tristan was using the additional light of his glowtorch to check for any creatures that might have crawled into his bedding and Jay did the same.

When he knew it was clear, Jay lay down and did his best to get comfortable on the thin cushioning. He hoped sleep would be quick to find him and that the only thing to wake him would be the morning sun. This was the only chance they'd have for an uninterrupted sleep. They were making good time, better than Jay had expected. It meant that tomorrow night they would be in Kada'rah territory and would need to keep watch over their campsite.

Closing his eyes, Jay did his best to fall asleep and not think about Tristan Fox.

* * * *

The next morning Jay woke before sunrise. He checked the perimeter but found no hint of the Kada'rah. He returned to their campsite to make a fire. Tristan was already climbing out of his bedroll and they shared a nod of greeting. Tristan packed up their bedding and secured it on the quaggas while Jay started cooking their morning's rations. Within twenty minutes they'd eaten and tidied the last of their campsite. Once finished, they confirmed their direction of travel and removed the hobbles from the quaggas. They were already on their way before daylight broke over the sand.

Unlike the previous day, they didn't fill the silence with conversation. They had crossed into Kada'rah territory and the additional tension left them both wary and on edge. The likelihood of being spotted by syndicate patrols increased and they had to be careful. They took things slower and changed their course if their sensors picked up any indication of Kada'rah technology. Jay often dismounted, using the cover of the high sand dunes to scout the area on foot. Tristan led both quaggas in his wake. The increased care caused slower progress, and by the time night fell, they had veered farther to the east to avoid patrols and weren't as close to the compound as they'd hoped. It was frustrating, but there was little to be done about it.

They established their camp in the shelter of a dune to keep them hidden from nightly patrols. The risk of discovery meant they couldn't afford a fire, so they used the light of the moons to help them set up. They placed their bedrolls closer together, with the quaggas positioned behind and downwind from them.

They prepared their meal in silence. It was when they were eating that Tristan broke the quiet to announce, "Cooking it definitely helps."

He was glaring at his meal and his displeasure made Jay grin.

"A downside of remaining undetected," Jay said.

He decided not to mention the others — like even with thermal blankets, if it got much colder, they might have to huddle together for additional warmth. They couldn't risk any heating technology with the Kada'rah so close. Jay squashed the part of him that was hopeful for that outcome. It was stupid and dangerous to give in. They needed someone to maintain watch, and a lack of sleep due to the cold would be a hindrance, not a help.

"Normally," Tristan said, "I'm meant to be seen but not noticed — or seen, but not discovered."

He stirred his fork through his dinner but didn't take a bite. Jay could make out Tristan's frown with the help of the moonlight.

"It's different not to be seen at all," he continued. "It's a sign of failure if you need to hide." He stabbed at his meal. "As it is, the attack on Zanik won't be looked on favorably."

Jay narrowed his eyes. "You'll get the blame for what happened?"

Tristan shrugged. "They will examine my actions and anyone else involved in the operation. I'm confident I wasn't at fault, but we will still need to be reviewed." He shrugged. "You know the ways of the system."

Jay did. Debriefings, mission reports and evaluations existed even on a successful mission, but when something went wrong — even the smallest injury — then the paperwork and examinations of everyone involved became three times more rigorous. A fine-tooth comb was brushed over everyone, looking for the smallest flaw or wrong decision. The scrutiny and questioning that Tristan would return to wouldn't be a fun experience.

"I wish you luck," Jay told him. "Hopefully the safe return of Zanik will help smooth things over."

"Hopefully he accepts my role as 'Bryce' as easily as you did."

Wincing, Jay asked, "How likely is that?"

Tristan's expression turned thoughtful as he tilted his head to look up at the sky, his gaze drifting toward Vicente.

"It's possible," Tristan decided. "I didn't hold enough trust for the deception to wound him too much — but he had started to confide in me."

New questions flooded Jay's mind about Tristan and Zanik's relationship. What kind of things had the Qui confided? How close had they been becoming? Tristan had said that he didn't sleep with his marks, but what else had they done together? Jay felt jealous, but he forced himself to ignore it. What they had shared didn't matter. It was how much Tristan liked him that was important.

Jay had never known the people he'd extracted, beyond a dossier. If a soldier cared outside the parameters of the mission, it could compromise things. At least, that was the fear of their superiors, but Jay had also seen when it worked wonders. A unit would go out of their way and perform miracles to rescue one of their own. How much Tristan cared for Zanik could be an asset, if it was handled correctly. The more he knew about Zanik and Tristan's relationship, the better he could judge things. And if it helped satisfy his curiosity and jealousy? All the better.

"What was he like?" Jay asked.

Tristan tapped a finger against his fork in absent thought.

"Zanik is excitable. Initially, he wanted to get me into his bed. He believes his father's influence makes him untouchable and desirable. The fact that I was difficult to impress was intriguing to him. He's carefree and naive and likes to tour his father's moons because he can always find someone who'll party with him. It makes him an easy target to get close to and" — Tristan sighed — "and an even easier one to kidnap."

"Did you like him?" Jay asked, feeling on edge about the answer.

Tristan hesitated.

"He could be annoying and ignorant, but he was occasionally entertaining. Yes," he admitted, "I liked him." Jay felt uncomfortable and disappointed, but it didn't last long before Tristan grinned, his blue eyes twinkling in the moonlight. "However, there were others on Vicente I liked more."

Jay smirked, his unease washed away by a surge of pride.

"A charming thief, perhaps?"

"Well, charming is still up for debate," Tristan mocked, but his tone was fond.

Jay laughed and teased the agent. "Keep talking like that, Tristan, and I might believe you *don't* like me."

Tristan said nothing but his smile grew. He turned back to his meal, but Jay still felt the warmth of the agent's words. The silence that fell was peaceful. Jay had never had someone he could sit with so comfortably. His platoon had always been loud and rowdy, and even when they were behind enemy lines, their liveliness never faded. Tristan was the complete opposite. He was calm and pensive, giving the impression that if one didn't keep him in sight, he'd disappear like a puff of smoke.

Jay might have missed the brotherhood of the UCAFD, but he'd also missed the companionship of like-minded people. After he'd left and turned into Jaybird, he'd never grown close to anyone. He'd formed no attachments or friendships. He'd jumped from world to world, never staying longer than a few weeks — until he'd met Bryce at the diner.

While Bryce had turned into Tristan, Jay's fascination had never stopped. Bryce had been cute and fun, but Tristan pressed every button Jay had and kept him coming back for more.

Despite the dangers and everything that could go wrong, Jay was enjoying being here with Tristan. He liked talking about his time as a soldier and enjoyed putting his skills into play. They fit together, and Jay wanted to see what else they could accomplish — but it wasn't that simple. He was a one-mission man. No one would want Jay to stick around. Tristan might only be a short distance away, but it felt like a canyon. Jay couldn't close the gap and odds were that Tristan didn't want him to. Jay could only ignore his growing feelings and keep moving forward.

Focus on the mission, he told himself.

"You said Zanik had started to confide in you. What did he say?"

"Nothing of much importance," Tristan said. He pointed his fork at a half-full moon. "They named Orvienna after his great-grandmother." He lowered his fork while continuing to list. "He's not as good with a plasma gun as he boasts. He wishes his father would trust him more, and he hates his older brother's adulterous wife." Tristan shrugged. "Nothing of use."

"Would he have told you more in time?"

"I think so," Tristan answered. "But Zanik wasn't my—"

Tristan cut himself off and Jay realized why. He had almost given away his mission objective. Jay was curious to know what IA had wanted on Vicente, but he didn't want to force Tristan to go against his orders. He quickly changed the subject.

"Did you enjoy being on Vicente?"

Tristan was noticeably relieved. "It lacked things to do, but it was nice enough." He cocked his head. "You seemed to like it, though."

Jay thought about deflecting. He could mention the bars the planet had or the sordid hotels that looked the other way about what their patrons did. There were the brothels and gambling dens or the industrial workers and tradesmen from Asam looking for a handsome, willing stranger to take them to bed. But none of them felt right, and instead, Jay said something more dangerous.

"I enjoyed visiting a diner with good food and an even better wait staff."

I enjoyed visiting you, he said, the implication layered in his words. Tristan's eyes caught and held Jay's.

"That couldn't have been the only thing that drew you back," Tristan murmured. "You barely knew him."

The moment was heavy and the air felt thick with acknowledged attraction, admitted fondness and ever-growing intrigue. Their night together on the IA ship had fanned the flames. Their time in the Carana Desert trading stories was pulling them even closer together.

"It was what I didn't know that intrigued me," Jay admitted. "All I wanted was to work him out."

"And now?" Tristan asked.

"I like what I'm seeing, and I still want to know more."

Tristan made a noise and Jay wasn't sure which of them moved. They came together in a fierce kiss and Tristan's dinner hit the sand as he fisted his hands in the material around Jay's neck. Jay shifted, trying to get closer and lean over Tristan but, suddenly, Tristan's hands were on his shoulders and shoving him back.

Jay's back hit the sand with a thump, grains flying around him and forcing him to close his eyes. When it was safe to open them, he immediately sought Tristan. The agent was breathing roughly and looking at him with frustration.

"We're on a mission," he muttered.

Disappointment overwhelmed Jay, but Tristan was right. They couldn't do this. He gave a jerky nod and tried to salvage the situation the best way he knew how — with a joke.

"I guess it would be too dangerous to have sex in the sand." His words fell flat and Tristan even shot him a glare. Jay held up his hands in surrender. "I'm not going to risk the mission if you aren't."

"I'm not," Tristan growled.

"Then everything will be fine. It was a momentary lapse. We won't let it happen again."

It took a few seconds, but Tristan's tension began to ease. He looked away from Jay, and Jay took the chance to sit up.

"We can't afford to fail," Tristan said.

"I don't plan on failing," Jay stated. "I want to get out of this intact."

Tristan looked back at him, pinning him with a heavy gaze. "So you can gain your freedom."

It wasn't what he'd meant. Jay had been concerned with getting them all out alive, but he took it for the escape that it was. He'd hinted at his feelings, and while he'd gained a kiss, he'd still been rebuffed. It was time to regroup. Jay pulled on a flirtatious, carefree smile.

"It will be nice to fly from planet to planet without a warrant hanging over my head. Hell, I won't know what to do with myself if I'm not looking over my shoulder."

"I'm sure you'll find something to occupy you," Tristan remarked.

"And I suppose you'll be reassigned far away from Vicente."

Tristan's cover was blown and there was no reason for IA to keep him on the moon. They'd probably never see each other again. Jay's chest twinged at the thought. He'd miss Tristan. Jay had visited him at the diner for weeks. He was a familiar, welcoming face. Even when he was scowling, he could still make Jay smile.

"Yes," Tristan murmured, staring off into the distance. "Who knows where I'll be next?"

Jay refused to let his discomfort show. He'd learned his lesson about admitting how he felt.

"I'm sure you'll enjoy no longer being a waiter."

Tristan rubbed his neck. "I would prefer it over a desert."

"It's not that bad," Jay disagreed. "I'd rather have a desert over a jungle any day."

"Oh?" Tristan asked.

It was the perfect way to redirect their conversation, and Jay didn't hesitate to expand on it.

"Have you ever been to the Hidici region?" Tristan shook his head. "It's a nightmare. Every planet's a forest. We once had to track a corrupt politician through it." Jay gave a theatrical shudder. "Never again."

Tristan quirked an eyebrow. "Oh? What was so horrible about it?"

Everything, as far as Jay was concerned — sudden downpours, constant bugs, large, carnivorous animals more dangerous than the armed guards surrounding the politician. The thick foliage and complicated root systems hindered even the smallest movement and made it hard to track them.

It was hell, but it made for an entertaining tale.

They both knew missions weren't all fun and games and that Jay was leaving out the darker aspects, but it was nice to go back to lighthearted banter. The Kada'rah's presence would soon require silence and stealth. Hand signals would be the only means of communicating. Tonight, their voices had to be low so as not to catch unwanted attention, but they could still talk. They pressed their shoulders together and curved their heads close, the longer Jay recounted his time in the forests.

Tristan even told his own stories — stepping foot on a boat for his first mission, despite never having been on the sea. Lightening his hair and eyebrows until he was blond to fit in on a planet. They had enough stories between them to last all night. They'd kiss again if they weren't careful.

They were having too much fun, and despite knowing better, Jay's eyes kept falling to Tristan's lips. He saw the agent doing the same.

But despite the temptation, Jay wouldn't let them give in, because he knew that if they kissed again, they wouldn't stop.

Chapter Seven

Jay took first watch that night. He couldn't sleep after speaking with Tristan, his mind abuzz with thoughts of the man and his own conflicting feelings. He tried to sort through them but didn't feel like he'd gained any ground when he woke Tristan for his shift.

They didn't speak and Jay crawled into his bedroll. His body responded to the familiar routine – sleeping the moment he lay down his head and waking with the smallest nudge to his foot. The night was broken by shift changes every four hours. Tristan couldn't be used to it, but he didn't complain. He did look more exhausted than normal as he woke Jay just before sunrise. Tristan drank his instant coffee like a man tasting heaven.

They ate a quick breakfast and packed up their camp. They knew they were off course because of the previous day, but it took them a few hours of riding to realize that they'd veered even farther off than they'd believed. They were nearing an oasis guarded by the syndicate. There were high sand dunes, which they used for cover as they dismounted and hobbled their quaggas.

Creeping to the top of the dune, they observed the area. The trees were thick and lush, while bushes surrounded the large, murky green-and-blue pool. Jay could see two Kada'rah members lazing in the shade of a tree. Their weapons were resting in their laps and their sandmobiles were parked nearby. There were hints of a campsite through the curve of the tree line, but there was no sound or movement to indicate additional Kada'rah nearby. Smirking, Jay looked over at Tristan and they shuffled back down the dune until they were out of sight.

The criminals were unconcerned about an attack, clearly believing that their post was an easy position that would encounter nothing but an unlucky traveler. It was the perfect opportunity to gain intel on the enemy's base and movements. They could even steal the Kada'rah's transportation to reach the compound quicker.

A rush of adrenaline and anticipation flooded Jay. It was a feeling that, no matter the risk, he'd never felt while thieving. This was what he was trained for, and damn, Jay had missed it.

Shifting to lie on his side next to Tristan, Jay used hand gestures to sign out the plan. Jay would make his way around the dune and sneak into the brush of the oasis until he could reach the Kada'rah and incapacitate them. Tristan would remain to observe from the dune and follow Jay down the moment the coast was clear.

Tristan confirmed the plan and Jay made his way down the slope to their quaggas. He circled the dune, staying out of sight. The hill of sand was large enough that he took a few minutes to navigate it. When he reached the lower edge, Jay checked that he was free from observation before hurrying across the sand and into the camouflage offered by the oasis' shrubs and trees.

There were no sounds of alarm and Jay cautiously crept his way over to the criminals. He didn't get too close, preferring to stay hidden near the base of a large tree as he observed them and waited for an opportunity to strike. It took fifteen minutes before the criminal standing against the tree shifted.

"Takin' a leak." He kicked the other man's boot. "Get up."

The seated man groaned but pulled himself to his feet. He waved off his comrade, who disappeared around the trees. The criminal put down his gun to stretch his neck and legs. It was a stupid mistake and the chance Jay had been waiting for. He pulled a knife from the folds of his clothes and soundlessly stepped out from behind the trees. He moved swiftly and used the butt of the knife to hit the man just behind his ear.

The Kada'rah jerked and lost consciousness. Jay wrapped his arm around the criminal's waist to keep him from a complete collapse. It was easy to drag the man back to where he'd been sitting. Jay rearranged him in the same sprawled position and cleared any tracks in the sand. He took the Kada'rah's main weapon before slipping back into the brush, choosing a spot that the other criminal would need to walk past.

Crouching down low, Jay waited for the returning Kada'rah. His breath was even and his body calm. Jay kept the sharp thrill of approaching victory tightly under wraps. There was still one more enemy to defeat. He hadn't won yet.

It took less than a minute for the other criminal to return. Jay grinned. The man found nothing untoward about his friend slumping back against the tree. Jay only waited long enough for the man to pass his hiding place before he was out of his cover and coming up behind the Kada'rah. This man was more alert and started to turn, but Jay was faster. He slammed one hand over his mouth to keep him from shouting an alarm before slamming the butt of his knife into the same spot on the man's neck. He went down like a ton of bricks, but this time, Jay didn't bother to catch him.

Moving him to the side, Jay removed the criminal's weapons and communicators. He also grabbed prisoner ties, which he used to bind the man's hands and ankles. He then repeated the same process with the first criminal he'd disabled.

Dumping everything to the side and out of their reach, Jay hooked one of the Kada'rah communicators around his ear before signing to Tristan that he was going to scout the rest of the oasis for any additional Kada'rah. He waited just long enough to see confirmation before he was off to search the perimeter. It was a large oasis, and it took Jay twenty minutes to circle it, but he was pleased to find no other Kada'rah. The amount of supplies, the lack of additional guards and the well-established campsite with a semi-permanent hut and two beds indicated it was a long-term outpost. The criminals wouldn't be missed for some time.

Returning to the two bound Kada'rah, he found they were still unconscious. Once assured they would remain that way, he gestured for Tristan to come join him. It took the agent a few minutes to unhobble and bring the quaggas with him, but when he reached the tree line, Tristan tied the reins of the equines to the nearby trees.

"What did you discover?" Tristan asked, coming to stand by him. He scanned the fallen criminals.

"Enough supplies for two people to remain here for a month," Jay answered. "There are no other signs of habitation. I'd say they're here to guard the area and dispose of any travelers who get too close."

"Travelers don't come into Kada'rah territory anymore. They know better," Tristan said. "Their lack of concern shows they expected an easy job."

Jay nodded. He pulled the other pilfered communicator from one of his pockets and gave it to Tristan, who hooked it to his ear.

"Their lines have been quiet," Jay said.

"Then we'll see what our captives have to say," Tristan replied. "The Kada'rah might not be willing to admit their secrets under interrogation, but untrained body language can speak volumes."

"The right flinch on the right question says it all," Jay agreed. "But even if it doesn't work, their sandmobiles are all we need. We can cut across the desert at nightfall and be at the compound in a matter of hours."

Tristan started tapping his thigh, his lips pursed in thought.

"We'll need to confirm the patrol routes and avoid them, but you're right. This will be our best opportunity to reach the area undetected."

Jay smirked. "Which means we get to enjoy an oasis for the afternoon."

Tristan looked amused. "While our enemy is unconscious five feet from us?"

"Better that than the other way around," Jay offered.

Tristan shook his head, but Jay had still caught a hint of a smile.

"Let's see what we can learn from them," Tristan said.

Nodding, Jay walked over to the first Kada'rah member and bent down. The man would have a hell of a headache from the knock to his head, but he'd suffered no other damage. He slapped the man's face to rouse him. The criminal jerked awake, his eyes wide and confused.

Jay offered a dark smile. He stayed crouched over the criminal, but far enough away to avoid a headbutt. He used every intimidation tactic the UCAFD had taught him. The criminal was groggy but quickly focused on Jay. He tried to struggle free from his bonds, but when the man realized he was trapped, he twisted his face into an angry scowl.

"I think we should have a chat," Jay said.

He lifted a plasma gun and pointed it at the man's chest. The criminal tensed and eyed the weapon warily. Would the man be sensible and tell them what they wanted to know or be foolish and end up unconscious once more? Only time and the interrogation would tell.

* * * *

The Kada'rah weren't cooperative. They spat curses, threatened to kill Jay and Tristan and refused to answer their questions—but Tristan was good at tricking information out of people. He used carefully worded sentences and verbal jabs designed to incite reactions. They could eventually confirm that they had relieved the previous guards less than a week ago. No one was due to contact the outpost for three days.

Once assured of their safety at the oasis, Tristan turned to the communicators. His familiarity with the Kada'rah, combined with IA's information, allowed him to work out the best time and way to reach the compound. They would go at night, using the cover of darkness and the Kada'rah's vehicles to avoid notice or suspicion.

Everything was solved and decided within an hour of their capture of the oasis.

When there was no other use for their prisoners. Tristan stood guard while Jay went to the storage container at the edge of the campsite. It held the syndicate's long-term supplies, and Jay pulled out everything that he and Tristan could use. He also removed the ammunition or anything that could be turned into a weapon. Once completed, Jay assisted Tristan with hoisting the two criminals to their feet. They marched them to the storage container and tossed them inside before bolting the door.

When they were safely contained, Jay surveyed the campsite. It was no longer a potential threat. It was now a perfect place to spend the afternoon. The large tent was raised on wooden planks and pilings. Its back was to the water and would protect them from the sun while giving them a place to rest. There was a fire pit they could light without fear of being discovered and the food the Kada'rah had was fresh and abundant. The Kada'rah also had a stockpile of weapons they could use to attack the compound. It was one of the easiest and most plentiful targets Jay had taken throughout his years as a soldier.

Turning to Tristan, he grinned and said, "Looks like we get to enjoy the oasis."

"Perhaps," Tristan replied.

His tone was neutral, but Jay could see the satisfaction in his eyes. It was a job well done, and they should reap the rewards. Yet before Jay could say words to the effect, Tristan stepped away and started exploring. Jay let his gaze linger on the man's fine figure before he went to the quaggas and brought them all the way in to the campsite. They shouldn't need the equines for the rest of the trip, but it was best to keep them nearby and tied to the tree with feed and water until nightfall. Situations could change on a dime. It was best to be careful.

After removing what they needed from the quaggas — both for their makeshift camp and the assault on the compound — Jay took a seat on the red-and-black wool rug that lay beside the burned-out fire. Tristan soon joined him. He had the keypasses they'd taken from their captives in his hands.

"These will get me inside easily."

"That's good," Jay answered. "The sooner you get Zanik, the less of a mess I need to make of the compound." He chuckled and nodded behind them. "But with the weapons we've got here, I'll have no problem creating a distraction."

"I thought the goal was to get in quietly?" Tristan questioned.

Jay held his gaze. "You never believed that would happen any more than I did. Slipping inside will be hard enough. You don't need them on their guard."

Tristan looked away, but his silence said it all. Jay was grateful. He didn't want to enter the compound at odds with Tristan. They needed to be on the same page to succeed and survive.

"We might have this sorted by tomorrow," Tristan said, his voice unusually solemn.

It was presumptuous to call a victory before they'd fought the battle, but they did have to acknowledge the possibility.

"We might," Jay admitted.

He looked away from the ashes to catch Tristan's gaze. The man's blue eyes were impossible to read, but Jay didn't need to pick out his emotions. They both knew what success would mean—the end of their association.

"What will you do when the mission is complete?" Tristan questioned.

It prompted a knee-jerk suspicion within Jay. Was he trying to gain information for IA? Did they plan to lie in wait and capture him all over again? Yet, as quick as the worry came, Jay dismissed it. He'd spent hours talking to Tristan over the last few days. He knew the man wouldn't sell him out to IA. Tristan had enough honor to stay quiet. So, he wouldn't lie, but that didn't mean he'd tell the full truth either.

"I'm not sure," Jay said, surprised that he really didn't know.

A clean slate would open a lot of doors for him, but his brief time in the desert had shown him how empty his life had become. He'd turned into a thief when he'd been wounded and wanting to spit in the face of the UCAFD. Jay had buried himself in the role, but he'd lost a core part of who he was too. He'd thrown away the good memories as well as the bad ones.

He'd felt more alive and happier on the mission with Tristan than he had in years. He needed to reconsider his options and plans. Major Chapman's exemplary record and his newly rewritten past would make freelance extraction work easy to come by. He could even set himself up as a bounty hunter and put his skills to work doing the right thing rather than the wrong one. Jay had a lot of choices. He just had to pick one.

"There's a wide universe out there to explore," Jay finally continued. His gaze fell to the rug beneath him. "I might check in on some old friends."

There were a lot of people he'd neglected, and there was one in particular who he wanted to see. Maybe, after this mission, he could visit them without feeling ashamed.

Tristan nodded but didn't reply. He stood instead and dusted off his pants. "Start the fire. I'm going to get some food."

Jay watched the man walk away, feeling confused and unsettled. Had his answer disappointed Tristan? Was he upset that Jay wouldn't be lingering around Vicente or signing up for a new commission? Jay hated that it bothered him. What did he care what Tristan Fox thought?

After turning back to the fire pit, Jay grabbed the nearby wood and lighter. It took a matter of minutes to get a good flame, and by that point, Tristan had returned with his arms laden. They didn't speak as they fell into the routine of cooking a meal. The food and drink were far better than a ration pack, but this time the conversation didn't run freely. They sat tense and didn't look at one another. The oasis was safer than the sand dunes, and yet they both acted like they were waiting for the sound of enemy fire.

Tristan finished first and stood without a word. He walked over to the raised wooden platform of the hut and took a seat. Jay watched him with a frown. Tristan seemed upset. Was it mission nerves? Did he fear what would happen when he was back with IA? Was he angry at Jay?

Jay doused the fire with the leftover water from his cup. The sun was high in the sky and Jay didn't want additional heat on a hot day. Standing, he went to join Tristan. The agent had sat down under the shade of the cloth canopy. His arms were resting on his raised knees and he was staring out at the sands. He didn't react as Jay walked up the steps and took a seat beside him. The air was cooler here, but Jay knew that wasn't what had made Tristan walk away.

Jay ran his eyes over the agent, trying to work him out. Tristan was as weathered and tired as he was after days spent under the hot sun of the desert. He had a sunburn forming on his forehead and the backs of his hands. Tristan was far from pristine, but it made him even more attractive to Jay. Maybe that was the problem? They'd tried and failed to tamp down the attraction that burned between them. Jay wanted him just like this — sunburned, annoyed and coated in sand. And judging by the way Tristan was swallowing and trying not to look at Jay, the agent wanted him too.

Jay knew it could be risky, but he didn't want to waste the few moments they had. They were alone in an oasis and they didn't have forever — only a small window of opportunity. Their mission could fail and, even if they made it out alive, they'd be going their separate ways in a few days. Right now, their mission was on hold. They were, for all intents and purposes, free to do what they wanted.

Jay knew what he wanted.

He shifted closer, his movement finally making Tristan look at him. They weren't sitting near enough to touch, but Jay's hair was on end, knowing how little it would take to feel Tristan against him once more. The agent wet his lips and Jay yearned to cover them with his own. He didn't see a reason to deny himself. There was no protest and no hint of resistance as Jay scooted closer then cupped Tristan's face and brought their mouths together. It was a soft touch, but it was charged with desire. The memories of their night together sent heat zinging down his spine, while affection kept their kiss from turning frantic. Every second felt precious.

When they broke apart, Jay didn't go farther than a few inches. His hand was still against Tristan's cheek, his thumb almost touching the other man's lips. They were both breathing more heavily and Tristan opened his eyes.

"Jay," he said, his voice low and rough, "the mission..."

It was a token protest and easily brushed aside.

"No one will show up here," Jay said, stroking Tristan's skin with his thumb. "You know this is a rare chance." *Our last chance*, Jay silently added.

Tristan knew it. Jay could see it in his eyes, could see the other man's mental debate too. It was obvious in the slight tension to his jaw and the small frown on his forehead. But before Jay could try to argue his case, Tristan surprised him. He closed his eyes and placed his hand on Jay's neck to pull him back in for another kiss. His decision was seemingly made.

Tristan's mouth was hot and moved with purpose. He nipped at Jay's bottom lip with his teeth until Jay let him inside. Jay groaned and slid his hands down Tristan's body. He got caught in Tristan's poncho before finding the man's hips. He grasped them and encouraged him closer. Tristan complied by climbing onto Jay's lap and straddling him. They never broke apart as they rearranged their positions.

Tristan kissed like someone had opened the floodgates, each move more passionate than the last. He ran his hands all over Jay, touching everywhere as if to memorize him. Jay matched the agent move for move, jerking his hips into the rolling grind of Tristan's and battling eagerly with Tristan's tongue as it curled around his own. He had one hand on the agent's neck and the other on his hip. Jay's world had narrowed down to Tristan and it was as if nothing else existed. He needed to feel those smooth, strong muscles naked against his own.

Breaking the kiss, Jay grinned at the sight of Tristan's flushed face. "You could use a few less clothes."

Tristan chuckled and mouthed at Jay's jaw. "So could you."

Jay angled Tristan back into another kiss before slipping his hands under the hooded wrap that Tristan wore. Jay fingered the material of Tristan's shirt before pushing it out of the way to touch his skin. It was warm and smooth, just like he remembered. When he scratched his fingers against it, Tristan shivered. Jay started to slide his hands up higher, but Tristan pulled away.

Jay frowned. "Tristan?"

The agent grinned. "I thought we said less clothes."

He undid the buttons of his poncho and yanked it over his head. His shemagh came next as he unwound it from his neck, letting it join the poncho on the wooden decking. Once finished, Tristan was quick to pull the hooded shawl off Jay and throw it out of the way. When it was gone, Tristan dived in for another kiss. Jay groaned and ran his hands up Tristan's back, bunching in the shirt and holding him close.

Tristan ground his hips against Jay's in slow circles as they kissed. It sent small sparks of pleasure through Jay, making his cock harden inside his pants. Tristan wouldn't stay still. He wandered his hands around Jay's chest, up his neck, through his hair then back down. He tweaked Jay's nipples and caused Jay to hiss.

"Sensitive?" Tristan asked before doing it again.

Jay would have responded, but Tristan was smirking and his blue eyes were bright with desire and laughter. It was the fun that had been missing from their first time together. It was as if someone had taken down a wall, leaving Tristan more open and ready to enjoy himself. Jay didn't want to do anything to ruin that.

"Only for you," he quipped.

Tristan laughed, and the sound made Jay's heart race. He let go of Tristan's back to cup his neck and pull him down for another kiss. Tristan came without hesitation, but he also shifted his hips. It let their arousals rub together. He moaned into Tristan's mouth. Their clothes were designed for long hours on the saddle of a quagga. They weren't designed for erect cocks. Jay wanted to get his free, but he also didn't want to lose the blissful friction that came from their slow grinding.

Tristan apparently had less trouble deciding. He pulled back and started to shift out of Jay's embrace. Jay held him tighter on instinct. Tristan just chuckled.

"I want more than this, Jay. I want" —he grinned— "to ride you."

Jay groaned and his hips twitched with want. The idea of Tristan on top of him made his mouth go dry.

"Yeah," Jay panted.

He ran his hand down Tristan's back and over his ass before cupping the back of his thigh. He couldn't wait to guide the man down on his cock.

"Yeah," he said again, feeling breathless with desire. "Any way you want me."

Tristan pressed his smirk against Jay's lips in a barely felt kiss then pulled back and climbed off him.

"Get the rug from the campfire onto the decking," Tristan ordered. "I'll get the cooking oil."

Jay couldn't resist a smirk.

"Yes, sir," he quipped.

Tristan rolled his eyes, but he continued to smile. Jay took a moment to enjoy the sight of Tristan so lighthearted and happy before he left to get the cooking oil. Jay forced himself up and climbed down the steps. He picked up the rug and shook it free of sand. When he came back to the decking, Jay laid it down. He was crouched beside it, smoothing out the edges when he heard the wood creak under Tristan's feet. Tristan stopped beside him and curled his long fingers into Jay's hair. He tugged softly and Jay turned to find Tristan's hips inches from his face, his arousal obvious beneath his slacks.

Jay licked his lips, tempted to undo Tristan's pants and free his erection. He'd only let the desert air caress it for a few seconds before Jay would take it into his mouth. He wanted to feel the way Tristan's hips stuttered as he tried to maintain his control. He wanted to drive the man *out* of control the way he hadn't managed on the IA ship. If he could get Tristan crying out his name and tightening his hands so hard in Jay's hair that it hurt, he'd consider it a victory.

But Tristan wouldn't be derailed from his plans. He removed his fingers from Jay's hair and bent down to untie his boots. Jay blinked his fantasies away and moved to do the same. Tristan finished first, but once Jay was done, Tristan placed a hand against his shoulder.

"On your back, Jay," he requested.

Jay willingly complied. He took a seat before lying down and looking up at Tristan. He could have felt vulnerable if he were with somebody else, but Jay knew he was safe. He could put his trust in Tristan and know he wouldn't regret it. That trust offered him the perfect view as Tristan pulled off his shirt. He stood there in nothing but his pants, the desert a backdrop behind him. Tristan was his own oasis — a beautiful jewel that Jay was lucky enough to have found.

Tristan stepped forward and straddled Jay again. Their arousals rubbed together once more, but it wasn't enough. When Tristan prompted him, Jay folded himself into a sit-up so that Tristan could slip his hands under Jay's shirt and pull it off. When the material cleared his head, Jay lay back down. Tristan looked gorgeous, leaning over him in nothing but his trousers, his cheeks pink from arousal and sunburn. Jay loved being at Tristan's command.

Tristan wasn't wasting his time or his advantage. He moved to Jay's pants, unbuckling and pushing them down. When Tristan's fingers grazed his erection, Jay bit down on a moan. Tristan responded by cupping his cock and giving it a stroke. Jay's breathing stuttered and he tried to thrust into the touch. Tristan chuckled before removing his hand entirely. He took his weight off Jay's hips so he could tug Jay's pants the rest of the way off, leaving Jay lying naked. Tristan licked his lips as he stared down at Jay's hard cock. Was he imagining it inside him, just like Jay was?

"Like what you see?" Jay asked, his voice heavy with lust.

"Always," Tristan answered, the honesty surprising Jay.

Tristan didn't look at Jay. He was focused on his fingers fumbling with the buttons of his pants, each second seeming to make him more frantic. Tristan finally removed his clothing, flinging each item away to join Jay's. When he was naked, he reached for the oil and poured enough on his fingers to coat Jay's cock. He stroked it and Jay spread his legs, giving him more room. *God, it feels good.* He grabbed Tristan's hips, needing something to keep him grounded.

Tristan's grip on his cock was glorious. Jay had always known the man had talented hands, but this went beyond Jay's expectations. Tristan interspersed slow strokes with fast ones, trailing his fingers over the head and down to Jay's balls. It could have taken minutes or hours. All Jay knew was his steadily building pleasure. He could have fallen over the edge right there if Tristan hadn't stopped. Something tapped against the back of his hand and he blinked open his eyes to find the oil pressed against his skin. Tristan was grinning.

"Make yourself useful," he demanded, a teasing gleam in his eye.

"Demanding," Jay muttered, but he was already smiling.

He took the oil as Tristan shifted to a better position. When his fingers were coated, Jay cupped Tristan's ass. The agent arched as Jay spread his cheeks and rubbed his slick fingers over his entrance. Jay pushed the first finger into Tristan and he let out a shaky exhale. His fingers jerked against Jay's stomach and Jay grinned.

He started a slow thrust in and out, stretching and teasing him with each motion. Tristan's eyes were clenched shut as his obvious pleasure sparked along his features. The sight sent lust rushing through Jay, curling low in his stomach. When Jay added another finger, he thrust deep and curled his fingers, searching for Tristan's prostate. When he hit it, Tristan's composure finally broke. He pressed his hands to Jay's chest, supporting himself as he arched back. He was clearly trying to get more — deeper, harder, fuller. It was such a beautiful image. Tristan looked divine as he lost himself to need. The way his spine curved at every brush to his prostate was more beautiful than the desert sky. Jay could do this every day.

Slipping his fingers free, Jay coated them with more oil before pressing back inside. He wasn't preparing Tristan anymore. He was watching the show. When he rubbed against Tristan's prostate again, Tristan shuddered and his cock jumped at the stimulation. It was weeping with arousal and Jay wet his lips with desire. He almost forgot about his own need to come. He was so busy admiring Tristan's.

"I'm ready. I'm ready," Tristan groaned. "Stop teasing me, Jay."

Chuckling, Jay removed his fingers, feeling Tristan's entrance flutter at the absence. Jay shifted his hold so one hand was on Tristan's hip while he brought the oil back between them. Tristan took the bottle before Jay could blink. He poured some on his hand before stroking Jay's cock and making sure it was well lubricated. Jay couldn't help thrusting forward, but Tristan didn't stop. He sped up and squeezed just below Jay's cockhead. He made sure Jay was good and erect before positioning himself. Tristan took a firm grip and guided the cockhead inside.

Jay moaned. His eyes fell shut and his head hit the wood as the tightness overwhelmed him. Tristan lowered himself at a slow pace. He gripped Tristan's hips and clenched his teeth. He wanted to thrust into the tight, blissful warmth, but he made himself stay still. Tristan was letting out soft huffs of breath every few seconds.

It was so much better than the first time. Sex on the IA ship had been cold, fast and impersonal. They had each achieved an orgasm, but it had been mechanical — two people going through the motions. Now, Jay felt like he was on fire, burning up from passion and want. He felt like nothing else in the world existed beyond the feel and sounds of Tristan. There was sweat on their bodies and the heat and smell of the desert remained, but all that only made it so much better. Jay fluttered his eyes open to look at his lover. Tristan's face was taut with concentration and desire and he was the most beautiful thing Jay had ever seen. Jay wanted to drag him closer and devour his lips in a kiss of hunger and possession. How had they gone without this for days?

When Tristan finally took all of Jay's cock inside, they were both trembling. He sat in Jay's lap, filled to the brim with Jay's shaft. Jay rocked his hips gently, making Tristan's voice crack on a moan. He fisted his hands against Jay's chest as he bit his lip.

"Ready?" Jay asked, his voice rough with need.

Tristan opened his eyes, and although it took him a moment to focus, when he did, he grinned. It was all the warning Jay had before Tristan pressed his hands to his chest and raised himself off Jay's cock before dropping back down. They both moaned and Jay tightened his hold on Tristan's hips. He drew up his legs, bracing them on the ground as he assisted Tristan. They began a slow rhythm of lift, drop and thrust. Before long, Jay sped up and Tristan rolled his hips to meet Jay's movements. Jay shifted himself to find the right angle to strike Tristan's prostate and Tristan cried out when he succeeded. His hands scrabbled for purchase on Jay's chest, his nails scratching Jay's skin and only heightening his pleasure. Jay concentrated to make sure he struck his lover's prostate every time.

Tristan started to curse under his breath, the occasional whisper of Jay's name slipping free. Jay couldn't take his eyes off Tristan. His damp hair fell around his flushed face, and his mouth was parted as he gasped for breath, his lips pink and bitten. Jay refused to look away. His pistoning increased while his heart pounded, not just from arousal but from something far more dangerous.

"Tristan," Jay gasped out.

Tristan opened his eyes. Arousal had darkened the usual bright blue and Tristan looked as close to orgasm as Jay felt—yet Tristan still bent down, disrupting their rhythm to press an open-mouthed kiss against Jay's lips.

Jay moaned and, on his next thrust, he pushed deep into Tristan. Tristan shouted and grasped his cock, stroking himself desperately. Jay raced toward his climax, cursing and panting Tristan's name, his desire rising to a precipice with no return. It only took a tight clench of Tristan's muscles for Jay's orgasm to overwhelm him. He came with a shout and arched deep into Tristan. Tristan followed him over the edge, but Jay only managed a few more thrusts before he was collapsing back against the rug. Jay let out a shaky breath as his legs slid down to rest flat on the wood. Tristan slumped against him, lying on Jay's chest and breathing heavily.

Jay lifted a hand to stroke Tristan's back in comfort and affection. It was nice. They might be hot, sweaty and covered in the mess from their activities but Jay still didn't want to move. The only thing he desired was to wrap an arm around Tristan and keep him close. He wanted to curl up and go to sleep with his lover.

He liked this. He liked *Tristan* too much. Dread formed like a rock in Jay's stomach. He looked at the man resting against him with the first wave of regret, because this wasn't a relationship built to last. It wasn't really a relationship at all, and any affectionate gestures he wanted to offer wouldn't be welcomed. Tristan only proved that theory by shifting off him and rolling away from Jay. He didn't go far, merely lying down on his back beside him, but it was enough. The sex was over and now came the consequences.

Jay made himself look away from the agent to stare at the cloth tent above them. He watched it shift with the breeze and wondered, *What do I do now? How do I deal with an infatuation and a wish to keep him?*

But there was no one Jay could ask, and there was no easy answer he would be willing to hear.

Chapter Eight

They'd shared a lot of silences over the course of their mission, more than Jay had ever shared with his platoon or other lovers. It wasn't that they could understand each other without speaking. It was because there were still too many secrets and walls between them to risk being honest.

Jay didn't know how long the current quiet had lasted, but Tristan was the one to break it.

"I've liked our time together, Jay," he said, his voice barely louder than a whisper.

Jay turned his head, but Tristan remained watching the roof. He was frowning, and while Jay wanted to wipe the man's frustration away, he knew it wasn't his place.

"I've liked it too," Jay admitted.

Tristan pursed his lips into a frown. He seemed angry, which didn't make sense.

"Tristan—"

"I don't know why you'd go back to being a thief," Tristan interrupted.

Jay hesitated, but he couldn't bring himself to lie or joke. "I never said I would."

Tristan snapped his head to the side. His eyes were wide, and he rushed out his next question. "Would you go back into service?"

Jay flinched. "No."

"Why not?"

"Tristan—"

"No," Tristan growled, his earlier frustration returning as he propped himself on an elbow to stare at Jay. "I don't understand why you would throw away an exemplary career."

"Tristan—"

"Something you're still good at," he continued, undeterred.

"Tristan—"

"And something that, for all I can see"—Tristan's voice rose—"you still love to do. So why—?"

"I saw an entire platoon get massacred, Tristan," Jay growled.

Tristan's frustration disappeared. His face became cold and steely, but his tone was soft. "What happened?"

Jay turned to stare at the canopy above them. He didn't see the fabric as he remembered the worst days of his life.

"The commander in charge was working for the enemy and wanted us dead," Jay recounted, his voice flat and devoid of emotion. "We'd seen something that could implicate him, although we didn't know that at the time. He sent us to capture an enemy base and save the hostages who had been transported there. He told us we'd be dropped into a safe zone with at least a day's journey before we met the enemy.

"The place was thick with trees camouflaging ditches built by the enemy to keep them from being surprised. It was a well-defended area, but we would have been able to take it...if the enemy hadn't been waiting."

Jay swallowed. He could still hear the shouts of confusion and cries of pain as they all scrambled to get out of the line of fire.

"They ambushed us," Jay continued, his voice becoming raspy. "The transport ship went up in flames. The explosion and resulting wreckage killed two of my men in seconds. They shot a few more down before we could get to the tree line."

Rage and pain were familiar companions whenever he thought of that disastrous mission. So many good men — *brothers* — had been lost because of one traitor in charge.

Tristan touched his arm. It was supportive and comforting, yet when he looked at his lover, he saw compassion and a matching fury. Tristan's understanding made it easier to go on. Jay didn't shrug off Tristan's touch, but he looked back at the canopy.

"A few of us made it into the trees. We tried to regroup and get to safe ground, but it became obvious that the information we had couldn't be trusted. It was designed to keep us trapped inside enemy lines."

Jay swallowed painfully. He could remember his friends dying all around him, the wounded knowing they wouldn't survive and staying back anyway to buy time for the few who were left. His team had been the best and had been together for years. They were a family and they would do anything to protect one another, even sacrifice themselves.

"I had twelve men," Jay whispered, "but only myself and one other survived." Tristan's grip on him tightened. "Milton was injured, and we took weeks to get back to the UCAFD." Jay closed his eyes, guilt clawing at him. "He needed a cybernetic arm. The damage was too extensive and the insufficient field treatment only made it worse."

"You know that wasn't your fault," Tristan insisted.

"No," Jay admitted, "it wasn't."

He didn't blame himself for deaths that he couldn't have stopped. He knew he'd done everything he could have for Milton — but it still hadn't been enough.

"They were my team," Jay said roughly, "and I led them there. I survived when they didn't."

Jay's survivor's guilt wasn't as bad as when he'd left the UCAFD, but he knew it would never truly go away.

Milton had been discharged, unable to remain in service with his cybernetic arm. Jay had returned with him to Milton's home planet, wanting to apologize to Milton's wife for not doing enough. She had hugged him and stopped him from speaking. She didn't blame him, and neither did the other wives and families. Jay had attended every funeral, and all they'd done was hug him. It made him feel worse and was another reason why he'd run away.

"What happened to the commander?" Tristan asked, dragging Jay back to the present.

"He tried to cover his tracks, but when Milton and I returned, we exposed him and the *dozens*" — Jay spat the word, still furious at the extent of the deception — "of people working for him and the enemy." Jay clenched his fists. "They're either in jail or were executed. The UCAFD tried to keep it quiet, but people still found out and took their revenge."

For a long time, Jay had wanted revenge too. Rage and grief had clouded his mind for years before he made himself let it go. He forced himself to accept what had happened and that justice had been served. Jay had been trained knowing that he and his fellow soldiers could all die. It was the bitterness of betrayal that made it so much harder to accept, but Jay had learned to swallow it down. He reminded himself that if he had died, he wouldn't have wanted his brothers to spend their life in pain and anger.

But it had made it impossible to stay with the UCAFD. He couldn't trust that all the parasites had been removed. It was why Heath had become Jaybird and why he had run so hard into a make-believe life. Jaybird only wanted a good time and a shiny bauble. He didn't feel pain or get bothered by betrayal. It was why being tied to a service contract for longer than this mission and why following commands blindly now made his skin crawl.

"I couldn't trust the UCAFD or the people giving me orders," Jay forced himself to conclude. "I still can't. It's why I work alone. If something goes wrong, I know it was my decision and that no one else will suffer for it."

Tristan didn't respond for a long time, but when he did, it wasn't how Jay expected. He moved his hand down Jay's arm until he found Jay's clenched fist. He rubbed his fingers over the knuckles, coaxing him to relax. When Jay complied, Tristan rested his hand over Jay's. He didn't link their fingers, but the warm weight of his palm was a comforting and grounding touch.

"What happened to you and your platoon was horrible," Tristan said. "I understand why you left." He squeezed Jay's hand. "Thank you for trusting me with what happened."

Jay nodded. He didn't look at Tristan, but he focused on the feel of their hands, the smell of the desert and the sight of the cloth moving above their heads. Tristan shifted onto his back again. He didn't say a word, and he didn't retract his hand. He remained a grounding presence until Jay could push everything back down and get his emotions under control.

Slowly, the memories of his past were locked away once more — gone, but never forgotten.

When he was ready, Jay symbolized it by shifting his hand from underneath Tristan's. He didn't want to pull away, but Jay knew he couldn't justify it any longer. Tristan's hand disappeared, but he didn't move any farther. They remained lying beside each other on the rug.

"I understand now why you would go back to being a thief," Tristan said, sounding unexpectedly resigned.

Jay smiled. He repeated his words from earlier. "I never said I would."

This time, Tristan caught on and he turned to look at Jay. "What *will* you do?"

'I'm not sure,' he'd said before, but now, after everything, Jay was willing to be a little more truthful. Maybe it was a mistake, but damn it all, Jay suddenly didn't care.

"I'll go see Milton. It's been a few years. I might become a bounty hunter." He let out a chuckle. "It's a legal profession, at least."

Tristan made a sound Jay couldn't define. He glanced at Tristan to find him frowning up at the roof. He looked like he was trying to solve a complex equation.

"Tristan?" Jay asked.

The agent jerked and glanced at him, but Jay still couldn't read his face.

"Would you be happy as a bounty hunter?" Tristan questioned

Jay didn't understand why any of this mattered. What did Tristan care if he was happy? Why was it important if he became a bounty hunter, a soldier or a thief? It wouldn't affect Tristan at all.

"I could do a lot worse," Jay said. "I might even end up loving it."

Tristan smiled but it didn't reach his eyes. Jay frowned, but before he could ask, Tristan was sitting up and the soft moment they'd been sharing had disappeared. Tristan was surveying the campsite with the eyes of a soldier. Their break from the mission was over, and Jay realized with regret that he should have kissed Tristan while he'd had the chance.

Shifting into a sitting position, Jay was shoulder-to-shoulder with the man. They brushed against each other before Tristan stood and grabbed his clothes. "I won't take long in the portable showers."

Tristan was about to move away, but Jay shifted and touched Tristan's leg before he could go far. "Hey."

Tristan turned and Jay stood. They were face-to-face and Jay didn't waste time. He leaned in and kissed Tristan, who instantly responded. Tristan's palm rested against Jay's chest as their lips caressed. The kiss was slow and deep, but it didn't last long enough. When they pulled back, their eyes locked. There were a thousand unspoken words lingering in the air. Jay hadn't meant to grow attached but he had come to care far too deeply for his mission partner.

"I'll miss you," Jay admitted.

Tristan sighed and nodded, gently stroking Jay's chest. "I'll miss you too."

Jay wanted to say something like 'don't be a stranger' or 'if you're off mission and hear about a new bounty hunter in town, come look me up', but Jay couldn't bring himself to voice the words. He knew what being a career soldier was like, and it would be even harder for Tristan. He was an undercover operative who couldn't afford to be recognized. Having a fling or a semi-serious relationship with someone like Jay would be a bad idea. He couldn't afford to have Jay in his life, not if he wanted to advance his career in IA.

No, if they ever saw each other again, Jay wouldn't be able to admit an association without putting Tristan and his latest mission in jeopardy. It was best to go their separate ways and never look back. It had been the plan from the start and there was no use making everything harder than it needed to be.

Tristan's hand was still on his chest and Jay was still cupping Tristan's cheek. Jay couldn't resist one final, parting kiss. It was just a brush of mouths but he felt Tristan's nails dig into his skin—a reflexive reaction when he recognized it for what it was—a goodbye.

They wouldn't be able to touch like this again. They needed to prepare for the attack on the compound, and even if they succeeded and reached the safety of IA, they couldn't be seen standing too close. The oasis had offered a brief moment where the real world didn't exist and nothing would stop them. But their moment was up and they had to return to reality.

When they broke apart this time, Jay didn't look at Tristan. He stepped backward and turned to face the undisturbed campsite.

"I'll keep watch while you shower," Jay said.

Tristan didn't respond, but Jay heard clothes rustling as the agent picked up the last of his things. When he had everything he needed, Tristan walked past Jay without a glance. Jay admired his naked form, despite the ache in his chest. Tristan paused briefly and it looked like he might say something, but despite Jay feeling a brief stab of hope, Tristan said nothing. He started walking again and disappeared toward the showers. Jay sighed and leaned against the wooden beams that kept the canopy in place.

"You always were a sucker for a pretty face," Jay muttered to himself.

But he knew it went far deeper than that—at least, for him. What Tristan was thinking and feeling, Jay had no idea. He also didn't dare to make a guess. Tristan wouldn't risk his career by being with Jay, no matter how much he might care. And even if Tristan were willing, IA wouldn't let a thief like him be with a promising agent like Tristan.

* * * *

Tristan didn't shower for long. When he returned, Jay stood without a word and walked past him for the showers, only taking the clothes he needed.

The campsite had a portable showerhead linked to a water tank with white screen walls that could be raised or lowered. There was a small wooden table beside it for resting clothes or a towel. Tristan had found two and left a clean one for him. Jay didn't bother with modesty and left the screen down. The cool water on his back was a welcome relief from days in the desert as he washed grime, sweat and the last reminders of sex off his body. He didn't linger, but he used the time to clear his head and bottle any lingering thoughts and feelings for Tristan. He couldn't afford distractions at the compound or to do something stupid when they got back to IA, all because Tristan had smiled at him.

After drying himself and pulling on his clothes, Jay returned to the main campsite. Tristan was sitting on the steps of the hut. His head was tilted so that his gaze could rest on the mid-afternoon sky. Tristan's black hair was almost dry and was curling around his ears. His poncho was lying on the wood beside him. Jay's wrap and boots were there as well. Joining him, Jay rested against the wood post that held up the hut. It kept a degree of separation between them.

"We have a few hours before nightfall," Jay remarked. "It will be a good time to get some rest." Tristan looked over at him, his expression inscrutable once more. "I can take first watch."

Tristan nodded and stood without a word. He stepped inside the Kada'rah's hut, where their beds were. Jay sighed and looked away from the agent's retreating figure. He turned his attention to the campsite, confirming that it was still secure before his gaze caught on the quaggas. Jay walked over to them with a smile. They had been munching away at the plant life and resting in the shade. He petted their coats and let them nuzzle his hands.

"I'm glad we've found a better place to leave you," Jay murmured, looking over the oasis. "IA might even pick you up the same time as they get the Kada'rah." He searched in the saddlebag for some sugar cubes to feed them as he praised, "You've done good, boys."

Brutus and Rinax made soft snuffling sounds, each trying to get closer to him in the hopes of more treats. Jay laughed and gave them a final pat before stepping away. They tried to follow him, but they were still tied to the trees and eventually gave up to focus back on the bushes they could reach and nibble on. Jay's smile turned soft and he walked back to the hut. He stepped onto the decking but paused when he glimpsed Tristan inside. He was lying on a cot, still wearing his clothes and with his eyes closed. Jay would have loved to join him, loved this to be their little shack in the middle of nowhere, a place they'd hired for some relaxation and fun.

Jay sighed and turned away, his good humor dimming. He sat on the steps and looked out at the sand dunes. They were numerous and ongoing, and the sky was nice and bright. He could almost imagine he was on a planet famous for its tourist traps — the top ten romantic getaway locations in the galaxy. Maybe the Carana Desert would become one, after the Kada'rah were run out by IA — assuming, of course, that was an outcome the security organization wanted.

Jay rubbed a hand over his face. It was useless speculating or fantasizing. He had a job to do. He had to stand watch. His weapons were close at hand and he arranged them easily, resting a plasma gun in his lap with his fingers near the trigger. It was easy to fall into a trance. Jay's mind was empty of any thoughts but the sights and sounds around him. He was ready to act at a moment's notice if something disturbed the peace and calm.

But nothing did.

Jay barely noticed two hours passing, but he twitched and turned when he heard Tristan stepping out of the hut. It was time to change shifts. Jay stood but didn't speak as they swapped places. He curled into the bedding that was still warm from Tristan's body.

His lips twitched as he closed his eyes and made himself sleep. It wasn't difficult, not with years of training teaching him to take a nap at any available opportunity.

Waking up was just as simple hours later. A small jerk to the edge of the cot made Jay jump to attention. He found the room much darker than before and Tristan was standing at the end of the bed. The agent was wise enough to keep some distance between them after waking Jay. Jay offered an apologetic look as he slipped the knife he'd been sleeping with back into its sheath. It wasn't uncommon to be accidentally attacked by a friend, as tensions ran high in combat zones.

Tristan waited for Jay to stand up and together they walked out to the camp. Jay rubbed a hand over his face to wipe away the last vestiges of sleep. The light from the setting sun was casting long shadows over the campsite while orange, pink and purple colored the sky in a gorgeous sunset. It was too early. They wouldn't leave for at least an hour. They used the time to eat a quick meal, pick additional weaponry from the syndicate's arsenal and make sure the captured Kada'rah would remain secure.

When they finished, Jay moved over to the quaggas. He untied them and pulled both the reins and saddles off them. He hoped that IA would look after them, but just in case, he would give them the best chance of survival. The animals seemed confused, but they butted their snouts fondly against Jay. He couldn't resist a final stroke to their foreheads before turning away. Jay joined Tristan by the sandmobiles. He double-checked that they had everything they needed, but when there was nothing left to confirm, he took his seat and slipped on the IA communicators that would connect them to the ships.

Switching on the sandmobile, Jay felt the familiar hum around his thighs before it lifted off the ground. The rush of air scattered the sand beneath him. Tristan raised his own vehicle to meet Jay's. Sandmobiles were fast and easy to handle, but they had their drawbacks. Unlike snowmobiles that traveled on the ground, sandmobiles hovered, causing them to radiate more energy. It meant they would be easier targets for long-range weapons. They were still fun to drive, though.

Exchanging a brief smile with Tristan, Jay focused on the feel of the engine beneath him and the taste of the desert breeze on his tongue. He pulled up his hood and covered his face while Tristan did the same with his shemagh. A moment later, Jay twisted his wrist on the handlebar to turn on the acceleration and the sandmobile took off. Jay guided it around the curve of the oasis and out onto the open sand. Tristan was a split-second behind him and the two of them stayed close as they sped their way across the Carana Desert toward the Kada'rah compound.

The sandmobiles ate up the distance, letting them crest the dunes with little effort. They stuck to open sand whenever they could, but the thrill of rising high only to drop low never failed to make Jay beam. The moons and stars cast a now-familiar violet hue over the desert and made it easy to see. It would have taken them a day, maybe two, to reach the compound on quaggas—but traveling late at night and cloaked by the syndicate's own vehicles, they took less than two hours.

The first indications that they were close to their target were the rocks that spiked up from beneath the sand and the additional greenery and wildlife spattering the landscape. They were reaching the foothills that the Kada'rah base was built into. The lights of the compound soon became visible and they brought their sandmobiles to a stop. They hid behind a large, looming rock that was twice as tall as Jay and wide enough to hide them and the sandmobiles. It gave them a good view of the compound.

The building lay below them, its gleaming metal bright under the moonlight. Guidance lights illuminated the landing bays and highlighted the men and women on patrol. The base was extensive and each building was connected. It sprawled outward like a military compound—but it was what was underneath that counted. Tunnels led into the mountains in case of attack, and like ants in a nest, their trails were extensive and impossible to pinpoint from the surface. Yet, unlike a military bunker designed for underground habitation, most of the syndicate's operations were held above ground, with the tunnels only used in an emergency. The Kada'rah weren't trained for an attack like a military force. They relied on their reputation and vast numbers to keep their base protected. It made them sloppy. They had bitten off more than they could chew when they'd kidnapped Zanik and prompted the involvement of IA.

Satisfaction swelled within Jay. He smirked as he scanned the area for potential targets. It might be dangerous, but Jay would enjoy bringing the Kada'rah to their knees.

IA intelligence suggested there wouldn't be more than forty Kada'rah members in the compound. An attack would draw most personnel out of the base, but Jay needed them all to come running. Tristan had to slip in undetected and have time to release Zanik and get back outside unharmed. He couldn't afford to be caught or interrupted.

IA would be waiting to assist them, but they wouldn't want to come too soon and risk the Kada'rah secreting Zanik into the tunnels. Jay had to trust that if they got into trouble, someone would come to help him. Forcibly shaking off his worries and his memories of the past, Jay turned to Tristan and gestured to the left.

The area was filled with large rocks, and when it reached the foothills, the terrain shifted to dirt and stones. It was a perfect place to hide and to sneak up on the Kada'rah. They didn't need to speak as they moved, darting between the rocks to remain unnoticed, while keeping an eye out for any Kada'rah patrols. When the sand gave way to the dirt and rocks of the mountainside, it became more dangerous to place one's footing. It was either a miracle or pure foolishness that it was unpatrolled.

They took a few minutes to make their way to the edge of the compound, crouching in the shadows as they searched for monitoring devices or Kada'rah members. When there were nothing, they used the cover of darkness to dart to the wall of the first building and press their backs against it. They edged their way along the metal until Jay reached the corner. He carefully checked for Kada'rah, but there was no one around. The compound was virtually unprotected because of that arrogance and the certainty that no one would dare attack them. The Kada'rah were used to the local authorities on Asam. They were clearly not used to Jay and Tristan.

Glancing back at Tristan, Jay made quick finger commands to explain his plan. He would go straight ahead to hide among the small fleet of sandmobiles. They would be the first targets for explosions. Tristan would creep closer toward the doors of the compound so he could slip inside during the commotion.

Tristan nodded his understanding and between one breath and the next, Jay was using a running crouch to reach the sandmobiles before anyone could spot him. The moment he was among them, Jay took a careful breath and let it out slowly. He detached himself from his emotions. Tristan was now nothing but another soldier to account for and protect. Tristan would do his job and get out safely, and Jay would listen for anything to the contrary. There was no time for worry or doubt.

Focusing on the sandmobiles, Jay pulled some small but powerful explosives from his pocket and strapped them to the energy cores of four of the vehicles. Their proximity to each other would trigger multiple explosions. Their destruction would also hinder the Kada'rah's escape via anything but the tunnels, leaving IA with a single target, should a search party prove necessary.

Jay set the explosives on a remote timer before hurrying over to a parked hovercraft. It wasn't the same one that had kidnapped Zanik, built for rough terrain as opposed to city driving. He attached another explosive but devised it to be triggered manually. He left the shadow of the craft to duck behind some unloaded crates. There were piles of them across the base, the ineptitude and laziness of the enemy serving Jay well and giving him dozens of places to hide. The many vehicles and ships created prime targets for additional fiery mayhem. They had offered Jay the perfect targets on a silver platter. He would have felt suspicious of his good luck if he hadn't known the truth. The Kada'rah had spent decades believing themselves to be the biggest, toughest and meanest thing on Asam.

Jay would change that.

When the first explosion went off, Jay grinned. It was a large ball of flame that caused all the compound's floodlights to switch on. Shouts of alarm filled the air, and the Kada'rah came running from every direction. Jay used the confusion to slip farther away from the explosion, planting the occasional device while he did. It took six minutes before he ran into someone. The man's eyes widened but Jay punched the criminal in the face before he could shout an alarm. He crumpled to the ground but Jay didn't bother picking him up or moving him. Jay only bent down long enough to disarm him before hurrying to another hiding spot.

His next explosion — the hovercraft — showed the syndicate that the previous mayhem hadn't been an accident. Jay watched from behind a stack of supply crates as the compound doors opened and armed Kada'rah spilled out in search of their attacker.

Jay knocked out five more Kada'rah members before his luck ran out. A female member was quick enough to shoot at Jay and he had to take more lethal action. But despite taking them out, things became more complicated. The Kada'rah stopped searching alone or in pairs, using larger groups and staying well away from anything that might explode. Some were shooting at the supply crates, hoping to give their intruder a taste of his own medicine. They weren't a skilled or well-trained enemy, but there were a lot of them and they had firepower.

Jay also had a duty to distract as opposed to killing whoever came his way. The IA was aiming for minimal casualties and numerous prisoners. They wanted an opportunity for interrogation. Jay did his best to maintain that order, but sometimes it just wasn't possible.

He'd been attacking the base for fifteen minutes when he tried to leave his latest hiding place and came face-to-face with another member of the Kada'rah. Jay caught and lifted up the muzzle of the man's plasma gun before it fired. The blast just missed him, but he didn't have long to celebrate. This Kada'rah was more skilled than the others, and while Jay wrestled the gun from him, they were quick to fall into hand-to-hand combat.

The man's fighting style was fast, full of sharp, brutal jabs of his fists. He had metal over his knuckles too, an item designed solely to inflict more damage. Jay avoided and blocked the man's punches, but he was being forced backward. The criminal was trying to corner him. Jay had to end that fast. He waited for the man to swing again before moving to the side at the last moment, and he struck the man hard in the neck, rendering him unconscious. Once assured the man wouldn't be getting back up, Jay scanned the area. The gunfire had alerted the Kada'rah to his location. He gritted his teeth before switching on his communicator.

"Trouble," he said to Tristan, turning back the way he'd come. "Move out."

He threw an explosive device behind him and onto a crate. It blew up on contact and kept anyone from following him as it dispersed the supplies in a mess of metal, food and smoke. He tried to head back toward one of the hovercrafts that hadn't yet exploded, but Jay didn't get far before he heard footsteps and stilled. Four men turned a corner with their plasma weapons raised.

They'd caught him. The one in the center had a ponytail of silver hair. It was the man who'd shot Zanik at the diner. His face was visible this time, and it was red with rage. He stepped forward, his gun never wavering from where it pointed at Jay's head.

"You would *dare* attack the Kada'rah?" he snarled.

Jay knew there were a lot of options he could take. He could surrender, plead for his life or go down in a blaze of heroic glory. But in the end, he decided on the one that offered the best distraction. He gave a Jaybird smirk and drawled, "Well, you made it rather easy."

The man slammed his plasma gun against the side of Jay's face. It snapped his head to the side and made it spin. Blood dripped down his cheek. The Kada'rah and IA communicators were grabbed and ripped from his ears. The man crushed them under his boot.

When Jay looked back at the man, the guns of the other members were still on Jay, but the Kada'rah leader had moved his to point it at Jay's knee.

"You will tell us why you are here," the man told him, "even if I have to force it from you."

Jay tilted his chin stubbornly and held the man's eyes with his glare. Whatever they had in store, Jay was ready to take it—for the mission, for honor and duty and, most of all, for Tristan.

Chapter Nine

The Kada'rah leader sneered at Jay's defiance. This man would follow through on his threats. The Kada'rah weren't afraid of torture. All they cared about was information and their reputation. This attack would be seen as a weakness and they would need to make an example of someone. He'd have to grit his teeth through the pain and find a way to escape — or hope someone would rescue him.

Jay didn't expect help in the form of an explosion. It struck another part of the compound and made the ground shake. The Kada'rah looked in the direction it had come from. That was a rookie mistake and they should have known better. Jay didn't waste his chance. He struck at the leader's gun, forcing it away from his body and punching the man in the face. He used the man's disorientation to spin him and put the leader in a chokehold. It forced the guy's back to Jay's front, turning him into a shield.

The leader struggled and clawed at Jay's arm, but Jay held him firm while edging them backward and away from the three guns still pointed their way. Jay didn't know how far he could get or if the criminals would still shoot him through their leader, but before he'd taken more than a few steps, plasma gunfire took out the Kada'rah.

"I left you alone for five minutes," Tristan said.

His unimpressed, exasperated tone made Jay smile

"I think it was longer than that," Jay grunted, still fighting to maintain his hold on the Kada'rah member.

"Release him," Tristan ordered.

Jay didn't hesitate. Tristan shot him with a stunner the moment Jay was out of range. The Kada'rah crumpled to the ground. Jay's smile grew and he turned to look at Tristan. The agent had discarded his poncho and had three weapons on him. Worry passed through Tristan's eyes as he searched Jay for injury. His eyes lingered on the wound on Jay's face.

God, Tristan was a sight for sore eyes. He was gorgeous and deadly with a hint of concern, even as he held his ground protecting Jay's flank. Jay wanted to kiss him — to hell with the battlefield and the danger — but they weren't alone.

Zanik came from behind Tristan. He looked worse for wear. The Qui's clothes hadn't changed since the kidnapping and his red hair was dirty and drooping around his face. He looked like any prisoner Jay had rescued, only he wasn't timid. He was snarling at the fallen Kada'rah, his sharp teeth bared. Zanik had a plasma gun in his hand and he looked ready to kick or shoot the bodies on the ground.

"I will find more," Zanik said, full of rage.

He went to walk away, but Tristan's words stopped him. "Don't bother. There won't be many to find."

Tristan's attention was on a device in his hands but he soon glanced to the sky. Jay did the same and saw a shimmer as the cloaking field was disengaged. An IA craft appeared overhead and IA agents leaped from it in jump-armor, dropping from the craft to glide to a quick landing on the ground. The moment they were on their feet, the agents had their weapons raised. They were a black wave rushing over the compound. The sounds of plasma shots and the orders for people to *'get down on the ground'* flooded the area.

The three of them were located within a minute, but it wasn't by IA. A group of four Qui surrounded them. They were decorated in the purple-and-orange swirls worn by the Taziv family. They were the family's personal guards. They surrounded Zanik while a guard spoke to him in hushed, worried tones. Five IA agents were only a few seconds behind them. One bent down to check on the fallen Kada'rah soldiers, three remained on the alert and the leader greeted Tristan with a salute.

He started a rapid conversation about what information was in the base, how many Kada'rah remained and what their next task would be. It was standard procedure and there was no reason for Tristan to hesitate, yet he still spared Jay a glance before falling into step with the other agent. He would be re-entering the Kada'rah compound to help strip it of information and technology.

Jay was left behind, feeling out of place and unsure about how to proceed. If it had been a UCAFD mission, he would know the steps. He'd be checking on his team, securing the hostages and prisoners and confirming their extraction was going according to plan. But with IA he had nothing to do. His role in the mission was over and the IA agents wouldn't want him sticking his nose in where it didn't belong.

Movement to his right brought Jay from his thoughts. Zanik and his bodyguards were coming over to him. Jay was wary, but Zanik looked curious, not hostile.

"I am told that you have helped me by choice, not by order."

It wasn't an exact truth, but it was close enough.

"Yeah," Jay said.

Zanik grinned at him. His sharp teeth could look dangerous to anyone unfamiliar with his race, but Jay knew enough to recognize the expression of pleasure and gratitude. Zanik placed a hand to his chest in a gesture of respect. "Then I am indebted to you."

Jay opened his mouth to protest but stopped. He wasn't a soldier anymore, and when he'd first agreed to this mission, he'd planned to utilize any favors or gratitude the Taziv family would throw his way.

Now, he wasn't so sure. Did he really want to get a few perks for doing the right thing? He'd saved Zanik because it cleaned his slate, but how could he have refused? The UCAFD had trained him how to help people, but he'd wanted to save lives since he was a child. There was no reason to take advantage of Zanik. He wasn't Jaybird anymore. The mission had changed things for him. *Tristan* had changed things for him. Their time together might come to nothing, but Jay was going to make better choices with his life. Zanik didn't owe him anything. Yet, before he could express that, an IA agent appeared.

"The ship is awaiting your arrival."

It was a command, not a request. Jay nodded and followed the man. Zanik and his bodyguards did the same.

Walking out from behind the crates, Jay got his first good look at the destruction they'd wrought on the compound. There were flaming wrecks where the explosions had detonated, while debris and spilled supplies covered the ground. Twenty Kada'rah were kneeling in the center of the courtyard with their hands tied behind their backs as IA agents stood guard. Jay could just make out Tristan talking with a group of agents by the doors to the compound. He was in his element—a confident commander giving orders that would be immediately obeyed. Jay forced himself to look away.

They were led out of the compound to where one of the IA ships had landed on the sand. The door to the craft was open, with two IA agents guarding it. Jay, Zanik and the Taziv guards stepped inside. The ship was a standard transport vessel filled with enough seats for the soldiers to rest but little room outside of the waiting bay and the cockpit. Jay took a seat without preamble, happy for a place to relax. An onboard medic noticed him and started examining the wound to his head. Jay let it happen. He knew how stubborn military doctors and nurses were. His wound was cleaned and healed by the time more IA agents were climbing on board. Tristan was with them. His gaze found Jay's but he was soon forced to look away. Jay averted his eyes as well, focusing on the entrance to the craft and the limited view he had of the compound. He thanked the medics when they finished and they left him alone.

Jay tried to ignore Tristan, but despite his best efforts, his attention kept flicking to the agent. He could hear snippets of conversation and the passing of orders. A few words caught his attention more than all the others, the timing for when the IA craft had revealed itself. It might have been a coincidence that Tristan was close enough to help him when he needed it. Maybe Tristan hadn't been able to escape with Zanik and needed the support—but Jay wasn't so sure. Tristan had stayed at the compound and had called for backup instead of leaving, and Jay wanted to know why.

Jay waited until the ship was in the air to ask Tristan. Everyone was sitting or gripping a handhold, but Tristan had detached himself from his entourage of agents and stood in a corner. His eyes flicked to Jay in obvious invitation and Jay stood and joined him, leaning against the wall beside the agent. They were close enough to show familiarity with each other, but nothing to hint at the depth of their intimacy.

"Everything running smoothly?" Jay inquired.

His gaze swept over the surrounding people, but no one paid any attention to them—or if they did, the agents were good at hiding it.

"Yes," Tristan agreed. "IA will strip the base of anything useful and the Kada'rah prisoners will be handed to the local authorities." He paused. "I've also informed the task leader of the oasis and the Kada'rah we captured."

Jay nodded but didn't immediately reply. He should care about the success of the mission and the capture of Kada'rah forces, but something else was on his mind. In a few hours, IA would have no further use for him. They would send Jay to a debriefing and he and Tristan would go their separate ways. Agents surrounded them, but this was still the best sliver of privacy they would get. If Jay never saw Tristan again, then he needed to know one thing. He lowered his voice, hoping to keep any eavesdropping agents from hearing them.

"Did you wait to call IA until you found me?"

"You said you were in trouble."

"It should have prompted you to get out of there," Jay replied. "You should have told IA and run."

Looking for me could have put the mission in jeopardy, Jay thought but didn't say.

"No," Tristan said, his tone firm. "Calling in IA would have added further chaos and invoked the Kada'rah's fury. It would have ended in your kidnap or death."

Jay swallowed. It had been a fear of his from the start. If the Kada'rah had been ambushed, they would have fled into the tunnels, taking Zanik with them. But it wasn't Zanik that Tristan had been worried about. Jay could hear it in his tone and see it in his face, the sincerity masking genuine fear. Tristan had been scared for Jay's safety. It wasn't the bond of soldiers. It was attachment and affection.

"Your mission was to make sure Zanik was secure," Jay whispered, his voice too soft. "I was meant to be secondary."

Tristan's eyes were turbulent with emotion and he shifted just enough to brush their shoulders together.

"I wouldn't put you second, Jay," Tristan confessed, his words barely audible but no less powerful.

Jay wanted to kiss him. The urge was so fierce that he started to lean forward, but Tristan tensed and Jay stopped. Tristan flicked his eyes to the side and Jay followed, looking at the agents. IA wouldn't remain oblivious to their relationship if they kissed in the middle of the craft.

Clenching his jaw, Jay shifted back to his former position. The air hung heavy with words left unsaid and feelings they couldn't admit. But before they could try to say anything else, someone was calling for Tristan.

They looked at the man who was beckoning Tristan to join him. Their moment was broken. They pulled away from each other as any remaining chance to confess disappeared. Jay pushed off the wall and gave Tristan a rueful, resigned smile. He followed it with a nod of farewell.

"Agent Fox," he said, adopting the formalities from before the mission.

He started to turn, but Tristan's fingers curled around his wrist. Jay startled at the touch and looked back.

"The common room of the ship is full of people," Tristan said, his voice fast but firm. "I always stop by after mission debriefings."

Jay was surprised. He'd thought Tristan wouldn't want anything more to do with him. Yet Tristan seemed hopeful. His thumb even brushed the skin of Jay's wrist suggestively before he let go and walked away. Jay stared after him as the man slid back into the role of Agent Fox—his face clear of all emotions, his shoulders stiff and his eyes sharp. He was every inch the professional agent—yet it was all a façade for his colleagues. He'd just invited Jay, a known thief, to linger on his government ship. Why would he do that? They'd said everything they had to say, unless he wanted to give them one final night together.

And what about after that? Jay wondered.

Jay dragged his eyes from Tristan and took a seat once more. He didn't look at anyone else. He focused on his hands that he clasped between his legs.

If he took Tristan up on his offer, would it be even harder to walk away? Would he barely get his clothes on before IA was knocking on the door and kicking him back down to Asam to collect his ship? Was it really worth one last hurrah?

No, spending another night with Tristan would only delay the inevitable and make the pain of separation worse.

So why, then, was he considering it?

* * * *

No one approached Jay or spoke to him as the ship made its way out of Asam's atmosphere and reached the IA ship orbiting above the planet. Zanik kept staring at him, but Jay did his best to avoid the Qui's eyes. When they landed in the docking bay and the doors opened, Tristan was one of the first to step out. Jay trailed after everyone but was immediately stopped by a new agent.

"If you'll come with me, sir," she requested.

At least they were more welcoming this time.

He was taken to the same room as last time, where the same man was waiting. The agent held out his hand and Jay shook it.

"Good to see you back in one piece," the man said before gesturing at the chair. "Let's get down to it, Major."

Jay took the seat as the man fired up a datascreen. The debriefing was short, to the point and involved signing five confidentiality documents and a letter that retired him from military service. The agent was polite, but he was still rushing him through every procedure needed to sever their connection. He should be jumping for joy, but the whole process made him feel unwanted, like dirt scraped off the bottom of a boot.

It took just over an hour, but when Jay walked out of the room, he had a clean slate. He was no longer a soldier or a criminal. He was free.

So why don't I feel excited?

The man shook his hand and gave Jay the name of an agent who would take him down to Asam. He wasn't being ordered to leave, but they obviously thought he would be keen to go.

Jay knew it was a stupid decision, but he asked to be taken to the common room. It was a short walk to reach it. The space was almost as large as the mess hall and filled with off-duty IA soldiers. Jay's escort motioned to a perky redhead. "She will take you to Asam."

Jay thanked and dismissed the agent but didn't enter the room. Freedom was at his fingertips, but Jay hesitated in the doorway. He searched for familiar, slicked-back hair, but Tristan was nowhere to be found. Jay tried not to feel disappointed.

The agents in the room were eyeing him curiously. They murmured to each other and Jay wondered if it was derogatory. They wouldn't want a former thief here. Normally, it wouldn't have bothered him. He would have walked in smirking and daring them to say something to his face, but now Jay thought about Tristan. He would be under investigation for Zanik's kidnapping and it wouldn't surprise Jay if people started questioning their relationship. His clean slate aside, Jay knew his time as a thief was a black mark against him. Jay didn't want his association to taint Tristan's promotion prospects.

If an agent saw them spending the night together, it would raise questions about their conduct during the mission. If Tristan's commanders knew they had slept together at the oasis, things could go badly for Tristan. He didn't want to be a cause of regret.

"Heath Chapman."

Jay turned to find Zanik approaching. The Qui's guards continued to flank him, but Zanik had showered and changed. He looked more like a confident party-goer than a rescued prisoner.

"I go by Jay," he corrected the Qui.

Zanik seemed puzzled before his eyes cleared. "Ah. Heath Jaycen Chapman."

Jay couldn't believe it. *Does everyone have a copy of my service record?*

"Jaycen Jaybird," Zanik continued, and Jay's mouth twitched at the new name. Quis were notoriously formal during first meetings. "I wish to offer transport to the Taziv home on the moon Scillakor. I wish to offer the gratitude of my family and to invite you to the celebration held for my return." He smiled. "My father desires to meet you."

His words wiped the smile from Jay's face. The Taziv were rich and powerful. They didn't invite lowly thieves to associate with them. In this part of the galaxy, an invitation like that was not unlike being asked to dine with royalty. It was an offer no one would be stupid enough to refuse—but Jay still could, if he wanted to. He could tell Zanik wouldn't be offended if he said he had things he needed to do on the IA ship.

But what reason did Jay have for staying? Another night with Tristan? A vulnerable moment where they admitted there was more between them than lust? A chance to ruin Tristan's reputation with IA?

It didn't matter if they'd formed a connection or started falling for one another somewhere in the middle of the Carana Desert. Life would only pull them apart. Prolonging it would make it more painful. The best thing Jay could do for Tristan was leave him behind.

An ache formed over his heart, but Jay ignored it. He smiled at the Qui.

"Thanks. I'd be happy to take your offer."

Zanik grinned brightly and placed a friendly hand on Jay's arm to direct him toward the docking bay. Jay allowed himself one final glance back at the common room, half-hoping he would see Tristan so he could explain what he was doing.

This is for the best. We both knew this wouldn't work. You deserve something better than this.

But Tristan was nowhere to be found.

Jay looked back at the Qui beside him. Tristan said Zanik was a guy who liked to party and was only in it for a good time. He was the kind of person Jaybird the thief would love associating with. He was someone Heath Chapman would have found amusing but would grow bored with quickly. Jay didn't know where he stood anymore, but maybe he could think of the Taziv party as the celebration of a new life and a fresh start.

Tristan was in the past, someone to push out of his mind and forget. He would give his attention to Zanik, revelry and alcohol, and maybe his mind would stop wandering to Tristan.

Maybe he could convince himself that he wasn't losing something important by letting Tristan go.

Chapter Ten

When they arrived on Scillakor, a large group of Qui greeted them. They all hugged Zanik and pulled Jay into firm handshakes. The entire Taziv family gathered on the moon to rejoice in Zanik's safe return. Jay was brought to meet Hezon Taziv within an hour of arriving. The Qui was a sharp-witted authoritarian, but he cared deeply for his family. His gratitude meant the Quis treated Jay like a member of the extended family. They said he could remain in the Taziv family home for as long as he wished. He tried to explain that he didn't want any favors and that they didn't owe him a debt, but it only endeared him to them. They considered his humility an honorable and respectable trait.

In the end, Jay gave up on the humble act and threw himself into celebrating with Zanik. The Qui could put the best UCAFD drinkers to shame and he never tired. He seemed unaffected by his time with the Kada'rah and saw the experience as a story to tell his conquests.

Sitting beside Zanik at one of the richest bars on Scillakor, Jay felt more alone than he ever had as

Jaybird. Surrounded by the Qui's personal guards, Jay allowed himself to get drunk for the first time in years. He hoped it would get his mind off the mission and Tristan—but it didn't work. Alcohol only exacerbated the problem, making his thoughts stay fixed on the agent.

Was Tristan under investigation yet? Was he thinking about Jay? Was he disappointed that Jay had turned down his offer?

Jay had a hundred questions on his mind, and it mortified him to learn he'd rambled half of them to Zanik while under the influence. He'd told the Qui about his time with Tristan at the diner, what had happened on the mission and how much he missed the agent.

* * * *

When Jay woke up hungover in a hotel room the next morning and realized what had happened, Jay wanted to find his ship and fly the high-hell away from this corner of the galaxy. Zanik showed up before he could leave. The Qui didn't suffer from hangovers and barged into the room while Jay was pulling on his jacket.

"You wake. Excellent. I have a fine gift."

Jay's head was pounding and he wasn't in the mood. "I don't need one."

"You must accept. I have transport waiting."

He gestured at the door where two royal guards were standing. Jay almost groaned. He still wanted to disappear and take his wounded pride with him, but Zanik was not someone who took no for an answer.

"Fine," Jay agreed. "But I need something to wake me up."

Zanik clapped his shoulder and laughed. "You need more to drink. We will get you used to the Qui way."

Jay didn't think he'd ever grow used to the 'Qui way', not unless he wanted to give up a healthy liver and sleep schedule. How the hell had Tristan kept up with the man while playing waiter?

Yet thoughts of Tristan made him fight back a wince. He had to stop thinking of the agent. Luckily, Zanik was a good distraction. He dragged Jay through the city, talking enthusiastically about the previous night. Jay tried to ignore him as he focused on the Qui version of caffeine. When he stepped out of the hovercraft twenty minutes later, the smells of the city were gone and in its place was grass and equine. He already had a bad feeling where this was going.

"Zanik, what did you do?"

The Qui grinned and walked through the front gates as if he owned the place. It was quite likely that he did. No one tried to stop them as they walked through the well-manicured gardens, past the various attendants riding or grooming equines, until they reached an elegant stable. Jay knew what was there long before Zanik presented them with a flourish. Brutus and Rinax were standing in luxurious private stalls beside one another. They made soft noises of happiness when they recognized Jay.

"Your fine steeds are returned!" Zanik explained. "No longer will you worry. The Taziv family will care for them for life." He stepped up to Jay and squeezed his shoulder. "Visit whenever you wish."

Jay brought up his fingers to pinch the bridge of his nose. He truly regretted getting drunk the night before.

Jay didn't know what he had said about the quaggas or how Zanik had found them, but he was glad the Qui hadn't gone looking for Tristan. It was a disaster Jay wanted to avoid.

If he had to accept a gift from Zanik to make him happy, a comfortable home for Brutus and Rinax was a worthwhile option.

Lowering his hand, Jay forced a smile. "Thanks, Zanik."

The Qui was bolstered and smiled widely. He patted Jay's shoulder and left him alone to 'reacquaint himself with his steeds'. Jay was just glad for some peace and quiet.

Stepping forward, he brushed a hand over Brutus' forehead and smiled at the affectionate nuzzle he received. Rinax even came closer to the edge of his stall. Jay had to stretch, but he could pat both the quaggas simultaneously.

"Well, boys," Jay murmured, "didn't you get a nice retirement package?"

There was no reaction, but for a moment, Jay expected to hear Tristan drawl something sarcastic — but the stables were silent and he was alone.

Sighing, Jay dropped his hands. He couldn't go on like this. Maybe it was time to put some distance between himself and Zanik? He should go to Asam and reclaim his ship. The sooner he had a way to leave the moons, the better he'd feel. The Taziv family were nice, but they were becoming a reminder he didn't want.

He'd spend a bit of time with the quaggas then he'd head down to Asam. There was nothing left for him on the moons but frustration and regret.

* * * *

Jay went to Asam that afternoon. Zanik had been disappointed but hadn't tried to stop him. Jay's determination to leave didn't falter until he was standing in the starport staring at his ship. The last time he'd been here, Tristan had been by his side. Jay tried to shake off the melancholy as he checked that everything was in order, but his ship hadn't been touched. It was exactly the way they'd left it, right down to the co-pilot chair, twisted toward the door as if waiting for Tristan's return.

Jay turned the co-pilot chair into a normal position and took the ship out of the starport. He'd planned to fly until Asam was a small dot in the distance, but he paused when he cleared the atmosphere. The IA ship was still in orbit. Tristan was there, somewhere.

What if he still planned to visit Zanik? What if he'd planned to find Jay?

It was a stupid thought. Jay hated himself for having it. It was a recipe for disaster, but he just couldn't leave. He returned to Scillakor. Jay didn't know what he would do if he ran into the agent, but he was infatuated with Tristan. He'd tried to stay away once. He couldn't do it again.

He would leave when the IA ship did.

It overjoyed Zanik to have him back, but Jay didn't spend much time with the Qui. He checked in occasionally, just to see if Tristan had visited Zanik, but he preferred to explore the moon. He'd avoided Scillakor in the past, finding it too expensive and arrogant for his tastes. Now, it was a nice change.

He visited the quaggas, sent a message to Milton and even bought a few souvenirs.

Three days passed and Jay felt like an outsider who didn't belong. He ended up in the cheapest, most rundown bar on the edges of Scillakor's main city. He was in a well-worn jacket with another low-brimmed hat resting on his head. The barstool was uncomfortable and the alcohol looked ready to poison him. Smoke from three different alien cigarettes filled the air. The low murmur of conversation gave the bar a secretive atmosphere.

The bar was perfect for Jaybird—but he wasn't Jaybird anymore. He didn't know who he was, but he didn't belong here.

Jay sighed and slumped over the bar. He felt more dejected than frustrated. Nothing was working, and he couldn't just shake it off or leave. Tristan was holding him captive, just like he had at the diner. Jay needed to know all hope was gone before he could turn his back on the man who'd stolen his attention and affection.

Jay was at a loose end, spinning aimlessly. The bar was perfect for his mood—dreary and not promoting conversation. It would get rowdy during the evening, but it was early afternoon and Jay would be long gone by nightfall. It was for all those reasons that Jay didn't expect someone to sit down beside him.

Jay ignored them, hoping they'd go away.

"For someone so skilled at hiding, I didn't expect you to be easy to find."

The familiar voice made Jay's head snap to the side. He stared at Tristan with shock. The man was surveying the establishment with distaste. He was in casual clothes—a long-sleeved gray shirt with the sleeves rolled up to the elbows and slim-fitting black trousers. He looked like a respectable, carefree tourist, but Jay knew Tristan would be armed.

"What are you doing here?"

"I thought that would be obvious," Tristan said, turning back to Jay.

It didn't feel obvious. Tristan wasn't dressed as an agent, so if IA had sent him, it was informal or part of a mission. Jay couldn't believe Tristan was there to manipulate him. It meant Tristan was here of his own accord. A shiver of anticipation ran through Jay. Was Tristan here for the night they'd missed? Would he finally be able to have Tristan spend a night on his ship? The thought was tantalizing — but Jay doubted he could be so lucky. Tristan wouldn't risk everything because of their attraction.

"It's not," Jay said. "Why did you come find me?"

"You didn't give me much of a choice," Tristan said. His eyes narrowed with annoyance. "Why didn't you stay on the ship?"

Jay sighed and looked back at his drink. *Now who's missing the obvious?*

"You know that was a bad idea, Tristan."

"What idea?" Tristan asked, sounding confused and hurt.

Jay took a small sip of the alien liquor. It was potent and burned all the way down. Here he was with a golden opportunity to be with Tristan one more time, and he was throwing it away. He'd been hoping for this very chance, but when it came, he couldn't take it.

Damn Tristan, and damn my conscience too.

"Us," Jay answered. Tristan repressed a flinch, and Jay tried not to feel guilty. "You've got a good career ahead of you, and you're a brilliant agent. I appreciate that you came and found me, but another round of sex before we go our separate ways won't help anyone." He finally looked at him and offered a sad smile. "You should be with your agency, not with me."

"That's the reason you didn't stay on the ship?" Tristan asked, his voice blank.

"There's nothing for us," Jay said. "You go back to your life and I'll go forward into mine."

"Oh, and what a life you plan," Tristan retorted. "Not a soldier, not a thief, but a bounty hunter. They're more hated than an IA agent on most planets."

"No matter what I am, I'll be hated," Jay rebutted. "And what the hell does it matter what I do? My past is still there, no matter how clean IA made me. I'm a black mark on a promising agent's record." He caught and held Tristan's angry blue eyes. "I thought you understood that when we were on Asam?"

Tristan clenched his jaw. "I thought there was something between us on Asam."

Tristan's words were a dare, a demand that Jay either admit the truth or lie about their connection. Jay was sick of lying.

"You know there was," Jay answered, feeling tired. "We both know that." Jay looked back at his drink. "But that doesn't mean we can—"

"No, that's enough." Tristan sounded furious. "I am not listening to any more of your self-deprecation and cowering."

Jay was shocked and offended. He was saving Tristan's career, and this was how he was repaid? He was sacrificing their chance at a relationship for Tristan's future.

Yet, despite his indignation, Jay found himself amused and fond rather than mad. He'd miss Tristan's blunt honesty. He'd also miss Tristan's frustrated scowl and down-turned mouth. Jay wanted to lean in and kiss the agitation away, but a kiss was the last thing they needed.

"It's not self-deprecation," Jay said. "It's the right thing to do."

"Since when were you concerned about that?"

Jay shot the man a glare. "Since an agent with an attitude made me give a damn about him."

Tristan blinked, looking momentarily shocked but he narrowed his eyes. Instead of a verbal reply, he closed the distance between them. Jay's eyes widened a moment before Tristan pressed their mouths together. Jay groaned softly and cupped Tristan's neck. Tristan fisted his hand in Jay's jacket and tugged him forward. The kiss deepened with a nibble to Jay's bottom lip.

It was the kind of kiss he'd been dreaming about for days. When he placed a hand on Tristan's thigh, Tristan made a pleased noise in the back of his throat. It made Jay's chest flood with warmth. He didn't want to give this up.

If Tristan didn't want to see sense and avoid a bad career decision, who was Jay to keep arguing?

When they broke apart for air, Jay didn't go far, staying close enough to feel Tristan's breath. Jay couldn't resist moving forward and mouthing Tristan's jaw. The brim of his hat must have annoyed Tristan, as a moment later, he shoved it away until it fell off his head. Jay laughed and nuzzled Tristan's neck, scraping the skin with his teeth and making Tristan shiver.

It was a bad idea, but Jay was past the point of caring.

"My ship's nearby."

Tristan was already nodding. Jay pulled away from the agent so he could stand. He threw down some money for his drink and grabbed his hat, which had landed on the bar. Tristan was only a step behind him and they quickly exited, their arms brushing as they moved. Tension crackled in the air and Jay wished he'd parked his ship closer.

It might only be his third time with Tristan, but his ship had one thing their last two hadn't had...privacy. No one would find or catch them. There was nothing to hold them back and no reason to look over their shoulders.

The walk seemed to take forever, but by the time they'd arrived, the energy and anticipation in the air had driven away all rational thought. The moment they were inside his ship and the door was closed, Jay grabbed Tristan by the waist and hauled him in for another kiss. Tristan responded instantly, bunching his hands in Jay's jacket as he pressed in close and kissed him with desperation.

The world outside disappeared as Jay slid his hands up Tristan's sides, admiring the muscles and strength in his wiry frame. Tristan skimmed his hands under Jay's shirt before scratching against Jay's stomach. Jay shivered and the kiss broke. Tristan rested his forehead near Jay's temple while he brushed the skin of Jay's cheek in a fleeting kiss. Jay ended up with his back pressed against the wall of his ship but the cool metal did nothing to dull the heat of desire racing under his skin.

"You once told me that you had a comfortable bed on your ship, Jay," Tristan whispered. "I'd like to confirm that."

The original offer seemed like it was from a lifetime ago, when they had both been masquerading as different people. It felt right to finalize it now, when they both knew who they were choosing.

"I'd love to show you," Jay replied.

He could feel the curve of Tristan's smile against his skin. It disappeared as Tristan stepped back, but he was still smiling as he waited for directions. Jay went to grab Tristan's wrist, but changed his mind at the last moment. He took Tristan by the hand and led him to the bedroom.

The ship wasn't large, and Jay's room was located near the front. It was designed so he could reach the piloting station quickly in case of attack or an emergency. The door to his room opened at a swipe from Jay's fingers on the control panel. It revealed standard living quarters with a bed built into the wall. The mattress was large enough for two and was unmade. The sheets were tangled and bunched at the foot of the bed while his bright orange-and-white throw rug was lying half on the floor. It was the only untidy thing in the room. His clothes were in the closet and his weapons were in trunks with locked passcodes. There was a bench with a lamp, covered in maps and logbooks. The rest of the room was bare. Jay's military training couldn't be more obvious — order and neatness of one's belongings was too engrained to completely discard.

It was the most personal place on his ship, and yet there wasn't a single sentimental item. Would that bother Tristan? Jay shook off the thought. What did it matter? Tristan wasn't here to debate his decorating choices.

Jay stepped farther into the room. The moment the door slid closed behind them, Tristan tugged on Jay's hand to make him turn then pulled him into another kiss. It was a slow, languid one. They had nowhere to be and there was no reason to rush. The affection that infused the kiss made Jay's heart stutter. He curled an arm around Tristan's waist but couldn't let go of his hand. Tristan looped an arm around his neck and linked their fingers. When their lips parted, Tristan was smiling.

"What do you think about being face-to-face, Jay?"

"Damn," Jay groaned.

Tristan chuckled and trailed his lips down to Jay's neck. He worried the skin with his lips and teeth, likely creating a nice red mark. It would be the first one between them. Jay tilted into the touch and let out a soft hiss of pleasure.

When he finished, Tristan asked, "Was that a yes?"

"Yes," Jay replied while bringing a hand to Tristan's hair.

When Tristan reached the edge of Jay's collar, he untangled his hand and started pushing off Jay's jacket. When the material hit the ground, Tristan yanked the collar of Jay's shirt aside to give himself more skin to mark, making Jay groan. He curled his fingers into the soft black locks of Tristan's hair, closed his eyes and enjoyed the feel of Tristan's hot mouth.

It was the first time they'd managed anything resembling foreplay. The IA ship had been a rushed encounter and the oasis had been plagued with the fear of discovery. Now, they could finally take it slow.

Traveling his hand down Tristan's back, Jay went lower until he could cup the agent's ass. He kneaded it and teased a finger between the seam of his ass cheeks. Tristan rocked back against him and Jay grinned. He gave Tristan one more brush of his finger before he went back to Tristan's shirt. Tristan hummed and he brought his hands to Jay's waist, catching the hem of Jay's shirt and tugging. Taking the hint, Jay removed his hands from Tristan. He dropped his shirt to the floor and Tristan's soon followed. When their chests were bare, they spent a moment admiring each other. Tristan looked gorgeous—but there was one thing missing.

Jay closed the distance and pressed his lips to Tristan's neck in a gentle kiss before catching the skin in his mouth. Tristan sighed and arched into the touch. Jay made the first of many love bites he intended to make all over Tristan before the day was through. Tristan's chest was next, although Jay was distracted by sucking on one of the agent's nipples. Tristan let out a soft, surprised moan as Jay lavished it with attention. He then brought his fingers to pinch the other one and Tristan's breath hitched.

"Jay," he groaned.

Jay smirked and continued to enjoy his teasing exploration. Tristan clearly liked his nipples being stimulated. He hissed and arched into Jay's touch. Jay gave each one final kiss and planned to move down to Tristan's stomach, but Tristan tugged at his hair.

He gently pulled him up until they could kiss again. It was so distracting that Jay almost missed Tristan's hands unbuckling his belt. His lover's fingers moved deftly, and when he broke the kiss, Tristan stepped back with a grin before whipping the belt from the loops. Lust rushed through him.

"Damn." Jay's voice was rough.

Tristan smirked and dropped the belt. He grabbed Jay by the waistband of his pants, tugging him toward the bed. Jay was starting to get a real fetish for letting Tristan order him around. While Jay wasn't naturally passive, he liked seeing Tristan's smile. He also liked the direction Tristan was leading him. Who was he to complain? He'd let Tristan call the shots, at least for now.

When they reached the mattress, Jay grabbed Tristan's hips. He stroked his thumbs over the material before sliding one hand down to cup Tristan's rock-hard arousal through his pants. Tristan let out a heavy gasp and pressed into the touch.

"It's almost a shame you want me on top," Jay murmured. "I wouldn't mind seeing what you'd do with this."

Tristan groaned, tilting his head back as Jay pressed the heel of his palm to Tristan's cock, giving it some seemingly much-needed friction. It took the agent a moment to respond, and when he did, his voice was deliciously rough.

"We'll try it next time, Jay."

Next time? Maybe Tristan planned to stay long enough for a round two. Excitement flooded Jay. Maybe they could make a day of it? Sex on the ship, exploring the moon in the afternoon... They could have dinner, and —

Jay cut the thought off and shook his head. He was not about to plan a date with Tristan. It would only disappoint him when the agent inevitably left. Maybe there would be round two or three, but he couldn't think that far in advance. He'd work with the here and now and see where they ended up.

Refocusing his wandering thoughts, Jay moved to the buttons of Tristan's pants. He used each button as an excuse to rub his hand over Tristan's arousal. Tristan's cheeks were flushed and his eyes had become dark with desire. When he couldn't draw it out any longer, Jay grabbed Tristan's pants and underwear. He tugged them down to reveal the man's beautiful, hard shaft. He licked his lips. Tristan's firm thighs and muscled legs were revealed next. The pants caught around his shoes, but since Tristan wasn't in boots this time, the agent kicked them off. His socks followed, as did the last of his clothes. Tristan stood naked and glorious.

Jay was tempted to drop to his knees and worship Tristan's cock. He wanted to make Tristan's knees shake and divest him of all proper thought. He wanted to make this a lasting reminder for them both. Perhaps he'd do it in round two—or maybe he'd use it as a temptation so Tristan would stay the night.

If Tristan were willing to stay on his ship, Jay would make it worth his while—hold him down and suck him off, flip him onto his stomach and finger him until he came again. Jay would fit in every intimacy the agent might want—starting with his request for face-to-face.

Tristan undid Jay's pants and Jay kicked them and the rest of his clothes off until he was as naked as Tristan. Their bodies weren't new to each other, but they both took a moment to admire. Tristan ran his fingers up Jay's chest, circled a nipple and rubbed over a love bite on his neck. Tristan looked pleased with himself.

Jay was about to make a quip, but Tristan placed his hand on the back of Jay's neck and coaxed him into another kiss. Jay closed his eyes and enjoyed the kiss as it slowly deepened. He touched Tristan's hips, stroking them before inching closer to his true prize.

He gripped Tristan's cock, making him break the kiss to moan. Jay stepped closer and fisted their cocks . They both groaned as he pressed them together. When Jay stroked them, it offered lust-inducing friction. Tristan hummed with pleasure. He sucked at the skin on Jay's neck as Jay continued to lazily pump their cocks. They rocked their hips in faint circles, but as nice as it was, it only left Jay wanting more.

Tristan must have felt the same, as after leaving only a single love bite, he pulled away. Jay caught his gaze and Tristan raised his eyebrows.

"Is that all you plan to do, Jay?"

Jay laughed and released their cocks.

"Then get on the bed and stop complaining," Jay answered, unable to hide his amusement.

Tristan looked equally entertained. His eyes were bright with laughter and lust. He took the few steps needed to reach the mattress. He dropped elegantly onto the bed, splaying himself in a way that made Jay's blood race and his cock harden even more, if that were possible. Tristan's legs were open in clear invitation and his eyes were half-lidded. His posture screamed 'come take me' and Jay knew the wanton image would be burned in his brain forever.

Jay had slept with countless people. He'd even had a few semi-serious relationships. But he'd never wanted someone as much as he wanted Tristan.

The man's cock was hard and curved toward his stomach. Jay's own arousal ached with the need to be touched. Jay climbed onto the bed, resting his body over Tristan. He kissed him, needing to taste his lips again.

Their bodies slotted together perfectly and Tristan hooked a leg around his hips, bringing their cocks flush. Jay groaned into Tristan's mouth then pulled away.

"Keep this up," Jay said, "and we won't get to the main event."

"Then hurry up," Tristan replied, his eyes twinkling. "I thought you knew better than to shoot early."

Jay was so surprised that he snorted with laughter. He pressed his smile to Tristan's shoulder. He'd forgotten how funny Tristan could be—or rather, he hadn't realized that side of him existed outside of Bryce.

Trailing his mouth to Tristan's ear, he lowered his voice to a rough drawl. "I'll make sure to aim where it matters, Tristan."

He heard Tristan's thick swallow and his smile turned wolfish. He pulled away and rolled to the side in order to tug open a nearby drawer and grab his lubricant. Tristan rearranged himself from his provocative sprawl to something more practical, allowing Jay to move down his body and position himself between Tristan's legs.

He planned to say something else—a teasing comment about where he was and what he could do—but he found his words stolen as he looked at Tristan's face. His expression wasn't one of unquenched desire or impatient need. It was soft and fond. It was the look of a lover. Jay stilled. The warmth in the man's gaze formed a matching tenderness in Jay's chest.

Jay was the one to look away. He knew that if he stared too long, he'd do something he'd regret, so he focused on their bodies. He stroked his hand over Tristan's leg before leaning down and brushing a gentle kiss to Tristan's inner thigh. Tristan shivered. He brought his hand to Jay's head, curling his fingers around the shell of Jay's ear. He rubbed Jay's temple softly with his thumb. It was the most intimate thing Jay had experienced in years and he closed his eyes at the swell of affection that overtook him. He tilted into Tristan's touch.

Jay pressed a final kiss to Tristan's thigh before turning his attention to the lubricant. He opened it and poured some onto his fingers. Tristan lay relaxed beneath him. He hooked his leg over Jay's shoulder without prompting, allowing Jay to arrange himself better, spread Tristan's cheeks and press the first slick finger against his puckered entrance.

Breaching Tristan was almost familiar and the agent responded eagerly to his touch. He grew accustomed to the stretch easily and was pressing back against Jay's now-three fingers in no time. His soft, encouraging groans accompanied each movement.

When Jay brushed Tristan's prostate, he arched off the bed and moaned Jay's name. He was stunning. His lips were red and his mouth was parted. His skin was flushed pink and his hair fanned out against Jay's pillows. Jay would never grow tired of the sight. He wanted to experience it every day. He wanted to spend weeks getting to know Tristan's body, as well as his personal habits and favorite foods. He wanted to spend months learning every quirk that made up the agent's personality, his likes and dislikes, his history and his plans for the future. Jay wanted to spend years learning Tristan Fox—but years, months, even weeks weren't possible and Jay closed his eyes against the wave of regret.

Yet, if he'd learned nothing else as a soldier, it was to enjoy what he had while he had it.

Jay slid his fingers free from Tristan, knowing he'd stretched him enough. He coated his hand and stroked his cock, getting himself ready. Tristan was watching him with the same contented smile on his lips. It made

Jay's arousal throb. It also made him want to forget his own pleasure to focus on Tristan's. He wanted Tristan to lose himself to bliss. Luckily, he didn't have to deny himself to give Tristan what he wanted.

Letting go of his cock, Jay shifted into position. Tristan assisted as he hooked an ankle around Jay's hip, encouraging him forward. Jay followed easily and placed himself between his lover's legs. Grasping his rock-hard member with one hand, he pressed the head to Tristan's entrance before pushing inside.

They moaned and Tristan tightened his legs around Jay's waist. Jay concentrated on sliding inside the heat and tightness of the other man. It felt so good, and it was difficult to take his time, but he wanted to give Tristan what he wanted. When Jay was fully sheathed, he pressed his hands to the bed on either side of Tristan. He buried his face near Tristan's neck, trying to keep his hips still. Tristan's hands were on his back, holding him close. It felt like a lifetime before Tristan tapped his fingers then slid his nails down Jay's back. The move was deliberate and Jay arched his back and jerked his hips forward.

"Yes," Tristan moaned, "again."

Jay drew out then pushed back in. He started slow, but Tristan dug his ankles into Jay's hips, urging him to go faster. He began a punishing rhythm. Jay drove his cock in hard and fast, gasping at the overwhelming pleasure racing up his spine.

"Tristan," he groaned.

Jay dragged his mouth over Tristan's neck and panted against his skin, rocking into every thrust and desperate for more. Tristan dug his nails into his back, doubtless leaving noticeable scratches. He pulled Jay closer, clearly not wanting a sliver of space between them. Tristan's cock was hard and leaking as it rubbed between their stomachs.

"Jay," Tristan whispered.

He nipped Jay's ear before he slipped his hand between their bodies. Jay shuddered, loving the idea of Tristan stroking himself off. He shifted to see Tristan's face. He was biting his lip and tilting back his head. Broken-off whimpers were escaping his mouth with every twist of his hand at the head of his cock. Jay wanted more. He started thrusting faster, aiming to hit Tristan's prostate every time. Tristan cried out, arching his back.

God, he's beautiful.

Jay turned his attention to Tristan's neck. He sucked the skin into his mouth, leaving a mark and making sure Tristan had a lasting reminder, even if it was only for a few days. Jay's own climax was building, but he wanted Tristan to fall over the edge first. He focused on Tristan, ignoring his approaching orgasm to keep up a brutal pace.

"Tristan," he murmured, "come on."

Tristan sucked in a shaky breath and tried to pull Jay closer. His hand was frantic on his cock and Jay knew he needed a final push. Jay shifted his knees to get a firmer position and thrust in at the same time as he grabbed Tristan's hips to pull him up. Tristan cried out and arched his body. His orgasm seemingly snapped through him like lightning. He clung to Jay and clenched around him. Jay kept his eyes on Tristan's face as he chased his own climax. It only took a few thrusts and he was coming in hot spurts, bliss rushing over his every nerve.

He collapsed forward when he was finished. Tristan's body was pliant and relaxed beneath him and he brought his fingers to Jay's hair, stroking through the strands. Jay hated having to pull out and lose the softness of the moment—but at least he didn't move far. He lay down beside Tristan, close enough that their arms and legs brushed. It felt good.

Tristan shifted, but this time he didn't pull away. He turned onto his side and propped his head on his hand, digging his elbow into the mattress. Tristan smiled at him and the expression was full of fondness. His hair was falling in little ringlets around his face and Jay wanted to reach up and brush them aside. He also wanted to cup Tristan's cheek and draw him into a chaste, gentle kiss. He did neither.

"Now what?" he asked.

Tristan's lighthearted expression suddenly closed off. "Are you asking me to leave?"

"No," Jay insisted.

He rolled onto his side and curled an arm over Tristan's waist, wanting to keep him there. Tristan relaxed at the gesture and his scowl began to fade. It gave Jay the confidence to continue talking. "No, I'm not asking that."

"Good," Tristan answered, "because I didn't come here just to sleep with you, Jay."

Jay frowned. "Then why did you come find me?"

Tristan eyes fell to Jay's chest. He looked unusually hesitant as he raised his hand and stroked it.

"In all my years with IA and even during my time at the academy, I've never met anyone like you," Tristan began. "You're talented and entertaining. You're attractive and smug." His mouth twitched toward a smile. "I work well with you and I don't work well with most IA agents." He looked at Jay again, and his former uncertainty was gone. "Your skills were wasted as a thief and it will be the same as a bounty hunter."

Jay huffed out a sarcastic laugh.

"Thanks for the compliment," he said sardonically.

"It's why I have an alternative offer."

Jay tensed. He felt wary and suspicious. With anyone else, he would have pulled away, but this was Tristan and he trusted him.

"What offer?"

"You don't want to be a soldier anymore. I understand that," Tristan said.

He was stroking a soothing pattern over Jay's skin. He was trying to calm him down, and Jay could already feel himself relaxing.

"You enjoyed the work we did on Asam," Tristan continued. "I can offer you that again. Become a consultant to IA." Jay's eyes widened but Tristan didn't stop talking. "You can choose your missions and we'll pay you for the ones you complete. You won't be a soldier with a rank. You'll be a civilian contractor who can leave at any time." Tristan licked his lips, a hint of his former nervousness returning. "You'll also be able to work with an agent of your choosing." A smile played at his mouth. "You'll be able to work with me."

Jay couldn't believe it. There was no way it could be real. He had been a last-minute option, an annoying solution to a bad problem. They wouldn't want to keep him around.

"IA couldn't have agreed to this," he said.

"They know a good man when they see one."

The other man's eyes were bright. He believed his words, and not only that, Jay was starting to believe them too.

"They're really offering this?"

"Yes," Tristan insisted. "The success from our mission on Asam and the reports I submitted have allowed them to consider you." He hesitated before adding, "I want to spend more time with you, Jay. I want to see what a partnership between us could create."

Tristan slid his hand off Jay's chest, but only so it could find Jay's on the mattress. He brushed their fingers together but didn't link them.

"You won't be tied to them or to me, but we can work together again. It's an offer to do the right thing and" — Tristan chuckled — "have fun while you're doing it."

It was a way for them to be together. Jay had looked at the odds and realized that their being separated was a foregone conclusion. Tristan had looked at the odds and reworked them in their favor. He'd seen potential and he'd found a way to give them a chance.

It was a hell of a leap of faith, and Jay could see how uncertain Tristan was about what his response would be. He was watching Jay carefully and trying to judge if he'd overstepped or angered him.

A part of Jay wanted to push away from the man and swear he'd never tie himself to another agency — but this was Tristan. It allowed him to stop and consider it.

He'd enjoyed the mission on Asam. He'd felt at home for the first time in years. He wanted to get to know Tristan and to give his life a better purpose, but was working for IA the solution? Could he willingly throw himself into the hands of another military organization? He trusted Tristan and he cared for him. Jay wanted a chance to spend time with him — but was that enough?

IA wasn't the UCAFD, but who was to say there wouldn't be fresh new traitors in their midst?

But you would be with Tristan. You would be helping people. And you'd be working with the IA, not really for them.

Helping people was what had caused him to join the UCAFD in the first place. He'd wanted to protect the innocent and defend the universe against hostile forces. Working as a consultant wouldn't be that different from what he'd done on Asam. He'd seen it while he was a soldier. Orders and command structures didn't constrain consultants. Their contracts were flexible, and they only went where they wanted and were needed.

It seemed impossible after a week spent wallowing on Scillakor, but Tristan had to have pulled a dozen strings to create this offer. It would allow them years to get to know one another and to decide if a relationship was worth pursuing.

It was everything he wanted, but it begged a very important question.

"Does IA know about us?"

Tristan shook his head. "No, but it would mean nothing if they did. You're not in the military and I'm not breaking any fraternization rules."

Jay nodded, letting his mind run over the pros and cons of the suggestion. The offer fit him like a glove and could give him everything he wanted. There weren't any downsides. It was perfect—and it was all thanks to Tristan.

Now Jay eyed Tristan carefully, trying to understand his thoughts and motivations, but the agent looked open and honest, filled with nervous tension and traces of hope.

Could he trust that the IA wouldn't screw him over? Not at all. Was Tristan worth the risk of finding out? Yeah, he really was.

Leaning forward, Jay brushed his mouth against Tristan's in a chaste kiss. He slid his fingers between Tristan's and linked their hands.

Pulling back, Jay said, "You're right. That's a much better offer than me being a bounty hunter."

Tristan's smile was small, but it held so much satisfaction and happiness. He kissed Jay again and shifted closer to him on the bed. They ended up rearranging until Tristan was comfortably on top of Jay. Their hands never parted and were twined together on Jay's chest. Tristan's head was on Jay's shoulder and he could smell the wood fragrance of Tristan's shampoo.

"We'll inform them of your acceptance tomorrow."

Jay's eyebrows rose. "Tomorrow?"

Tristan was amused. "I asked for twenty-four hours' shore leave. I plan to use every hour of it, Jay. In fact, didn't you say something about a bit of a role reversal the next time?"

Laughing, Jay ran his hand over Tristan's back. He delighted in the fact that he could do it without fear of who might see them or when Tristan might leave. They had all the time in the world now to explore each other and see how they fit together.

"Tell me more about those plans, Agent Fox," Jay said, a smirk curling his lips. "We'll see if I can't improve on them."

Want to see more from this author?
Here's a taster for you to enjoy!

Hard Evidence:
Ticket to Freedom
Elizabeth Hollows

Excerpt

Calvin Hughes opened the alleyway door with gritted teeth and a shudder. It closed behind him and he took in a grateful breath of clean air. Well, cleaner air. It was free from cigarette smoke and alcohol fumes, but there was a large, overflowing bin next to him. Calvin curled his lip and stood as far away from it as possible. He didn't lean up against the damp wall, choosing instead to stare out at the street. Neon lights bathed the busy sidewalk in red, blue and green.

The neighborhood was more than sleazy. It was downright criminal.

Calvin worked in a dive bar that was a front for all manner of illegal dealings, but he didn't get involved. He kept his head down and poured drinks. People who paid too much attention or spoke out of turn ended up with bruises and broken bones. Sometimes they disappeared entirely. It wasn't the life or career he wanted, but he had been down on his luck and desperate for a job. The bar had hired him when no one else would. Three years ago, Calvin hadn't known what dangers lurked in the shadows. Now he was stuck. He wanted to quit but was fearful of what would happen if he did.

He was lucky the patrons liked to fondle the waitresses rather than the quiet man behind the bar. He didn't even advertise he was gay. Calvin didn't want to catch the eye of a criminal who would take his sexuality as an open invitation. Luckily, there weren't many handsome men to interest him. The few attractive ones were arrogant, cruel or unquestionably straight.

Calvin had given up hoping for a knight in shining armor years ago. He was stuck, and no one would rescue him.

Sighing, Calvin looked up at the sky. It was overcast and there was too much light pollution to see the stars. He missed the country. He'd grown up in a small town in the middle of nowhere. What he wouldn't give for a one-way ticket back there—a one-way ticket to anywhere else, somewhere with a small house, a loving dog, maybe even a loving husband. He could dream.

And, that was what Calvin did on his five-minute break. He daydreamed about the perfect life—a man wrapping his warm, strong arms around Calvin and kissing him breathless, nights of passion in bed and mornings spent cooking together. The images were sweet, even if they made the bar seem darker and gloomier by comparison.

Sighing again, Calvin glanced at his watch. It didn't pay to be late in a place like this. He was lucky he had a break at all. His bosses didn't care much about worker's rights.

Calvin let go of his fantasy man with regret and turned back to the door. He reached for the handle but flinched away at the muffled sounds of shouting and a gunshot. His blood ran cold, but before he could react, the door burst open and someone collided with him. Calvin grabbed onto the man to keep his footing, only narrowly avoiding falling to the ground. He looked down at the man in his arms. He was brunet and few inches shorter than Calvin. *Felix.* He was one of the few handsome faces Calvin saw. He didn't treat the waitstaff like dirt and had an infectious smile.

Felix had been coming into the club for the last month and a half. He ordered a beer but never drank it. He flirted with the barmaids and schmoozed with the owners. Calvin had seen him exchanging money. He'd also been part of private meetings in the back room. Felix wasn't deep into the illegal dealings, but he'd been worming his way into the inner circle. Felix was a young, up-and-rising criminal star. Calvin stayed away from people like that, no matter how handsome they were in a well-tailored suit.

Felix's suit was in disarray now and his blue eyes were almost wild. The door had slammed shut behind him, but they both ducked when a new shot was fired. It penetrated the door but missed them.

Felix yanked Calvin farther down the alley and away from the door. He let Calvin go when they turned a corner but didn't stop running. Calvin raced after him. They sprinted behind the buildings and past two exits to the street. Felix kept going until they reached a narrow road with a parked car. Calvin could still hear shouting, screaming and running footsteps. They seemed to be echoing all around them. Felix unlocked the car and jumped inside. Calvin didn't think about what he was doing. He yanked open the passenger door then climbed in.

"What the hell?" Felix shouted. "Get out of here!"

He threw something on the backseat, but before Calvin could react, another gunshot from behind shattered the back windshield. Calvin cried out and ducked forward. The car roared to life and they tore out onto the street. Calvin snapped up his head, yelping with terror when they narrowly avoided a collision with another car. Felix didn't blink, skidding the tires and twisting the wheel to make it through without a scratch. Felix put his foot down on the accelerator, flying at three times the speed limit and weaving in and out of cars like a maniac.

Calvin's heart was pounding and he was ready to be sick by the time they screeched onto the main highway. The dive bars and nightclubs were disappearing, but Felix didn't slow down. He kept checking the rearview and side mirrors making sure they weren't being followed. Calvin panted heavily and tried to calm his racing heart. It wasn't working.

He didn't know what was going on, but Calvin had the sinking suspicion he shouldn't have climbed into this car. He tentatively turned and looked behind him. Glass from the shattered window littered the backseat. Another item rested on the cushioning and Calvin's eyes widened.

"You stole the hard drive," he whispered.

Calvin had only seen the hard drive four times, but he would know it anywhere.

Whenever the bar was short-staffed or the waitresses had gone home, Calvin took drinks to the back room of the club. Calvin tried to be inconspicuous while he was there. He presented drinks to the table of men playing cards. It was a simple activity that masked horrible intentions. Only the top men and women were invited to that game. Murders and drug deals were planned in that room and every few months, a black laptop rested on the table. Calvin didn't want to know what information was on it. There was always a hard drive plugged into the computer. It was a small silver one with a scratch in the corner.

It was the same hard drive that rested under broken glass on Felix's back seat. He turned back to find Felix clenching the steering wheel and gritting his teeth.

"You stole the hard drive," Calvin said again, his voice growing louder and threaded with panic.

"Why the hell did you get in my car?" Felix snapped. "What the hell were you doing?"

Calvin hadn't been thinking and that was the problem. Felix had pulled him away from the door and the gunshots. He'd assumed Felix would be safe or at least unconnected with what was going on in the club. He'd been wrong.

Now, Calvin was in a car with the man everyone wanted to see dead. He was guilty by association.

I'm screwed.

"Well?" Felix demanded, glancing away from the road to glare at him. "Got any more stupid ideas?"

Calvin bristled at the insult.

"You pulled me away from the door! How was I supposed to know you were the one they were shooting at?"

"What kind of idiot jumps into a car with a stranger?"

"What kind of idiot steals a hard drive from a criminal empire?"

Felix clenched his jaw but didn't respond. Calvin was breathing heavily, adrenaline pumping through his veins and making his hands tremble. He turned away from Felix to stare out of the window. They were still in the city with cars, buildings and people all around them. It didn't comfort him.

Where is Felix taking us? Where is he taking the hard drive?

There were hundreds of rival gangs and organizations that would love to have that hard drive.

How much danger am I in right now? Is Felix going to silence me before I can talk to anyone?

Calvin knew it was useless, but as the terror took hold again, he found words tumbling out of him.

"I won't tell anyone if you let me go. They won't know anything, I swear."

Felix startled, seeming surprised by his statement. "Let you go? You'll be dead within hours if I let you go."

A cold shiver of fear ran down Calvin's spine. It was one thing to think it, another to hear it.

PUBLISHING

Sign up for our newsletter and find out about all our
romance book releases, eBook sales and promotions,
sneak peeks and FREE romance books!

About the Author

Elizabeth Hollows is an Australian writer of LGBT love stories specializing in homosexual or lesbian romance. Her preferred genres are fantasy, science fiction and contemporary/modern.

She has been writing since she was twelve, but has spent the last few years writing romance stories and discovering a passion for LGBT romance.

When Elizabeth is not writing she embroiders, reads and plots her next novel. She is a fan of the winter months and always has a book in her handbag and a cup of tea nearby.

Elizabeth loves to hear from readers. You can find her contact information, website details and author profile page at https://www.pride-publishing.com